Margaret E. Winslow

Sketch of the Life, Character and Work of Alonzo Crittenden

Late President of the Packer Collegiate Institute

Margaret E. Winslow

Sketch of the Life, Character and Work of Alonzo Crittenden
Late President of the Packer Collegiate Institute

ISBN/EAN: 9783337097783

Printed in Europe, USA, Canada, Australia, Japan

Cover: Foto ©Raphael Reischuk / pixelio.de

More available books at **www.hansebooks.com**

SKETCH

OF THE

LIFE, CHARACTER AND WORK

OF

ALONZO CRITTENDEN, A.M., Ph.D.

LATE PRESIDENT

OF THE

PACKER COLLEGIATE INSTITUTE

EDITED BY

MARGARET E. WINSLOW

NEW YORK
A. S. BARNES & CO.
1885

INTRODUCTION.

THE following Memoir of the life and character of the late ALONZO CRITTENDEN, Ph.D., is published under the auspices of the Board of Trustees of the Packer Collegiate Institute, of which till the time of his death he was the honored Principal.

It has been the primal aim of its Author to present to the reader a true likeness of this excellent man, just as he stood, day by day, for sixty years, before teachers and scholars, an animating and inspiring presence, commanding the respect of all as a faithful guardian, guide, and friend.

To hundreds and thousands of those who have been associated with him in a work which he so much loved, or have profited by his instructions in the several Institutions over which he presided, such an aid to memory as this book affords must possess an abiding interest.

In calling to recollection the traits of character that distinguished Doctor CRITTENDEN in his educational life, the testimony of those who were co-workers with him has been freely supplied: while others whom he led in the paths of knowledge bear concurrent witness to the vigilance and vigor of his administration, and to the happy impress made upon the heart by the high moral purpose which he steadfastly enforced.

In the course of the following narrative the felicities of his home—a home that divided with the school the affections of his warm and loving heart—are brought conspicuously to view, as well as the beautiful hospitality that characterized his rural retirement.

For him the country had many charms, and his love of nature and his love of friends combined to make his hospitality delightful to all who were privileged to visit him.

This interesting volume closes with the words of eulogy so happily spoken by the various clergymen of our own and the neighboring city, and with appropriate resolutions adopted by Boards of Trustees, of this and other Institutions, at the time of his death.

A. A. Low,
President of the Board of Trustees.

Brooklyn, March 10, 1885.

CONTENTS.

CHAPTER I.

EARLY DAYS.

PAGE

Parentage—Birth — Childhood — Education—College Life —
Goes to Albany—Mary Warner—Marriage—Offspring, . 9

CHAPTER II.

THE ALBANY FEMALE ACADEMY.

Reminiscences of Old Scholars—Appreciation of the Trustees
— Professor Horsford's Memories—Dr. CRITTENDEN'S
Account —Tribute of Pupils, ... 27

CHAPTER III.

THE BROOKLYN FEMALE ACADEMY.

Call for Meeting of Citizens—Invitation to Dr. CRITTENDEN
—Letter of Acceptance—Move to Brooklyn—Professor
Alonzo Gray—Academy Built—Opening—The Principal—
The Library—Anecdotes, ... 42

CHAPTER IV.

LAST DAYS OF THE ACADEMY.

Discipline—An Old Teacher—Religious Influence—Dr. Spencer—Sorrows—A Change of Professors—The Fire, . . 60

CHAPTER V.

THE PACKER COLLEGIATE INSTITUTE.

PAGE

A Generous Offer—Erection of the Building—Dedication—
Golden Years—Financial Ability—Principles of Government—Anecdotes, ... 74

CHAPTER VI,

TRAITS OF CHARACTER.

Quick Intuition—Constancy of Friendship—Revivalist—Unlimited Power of Forgiveness—Story of Two Sisters—
Judicious Charity—Repartee—Illustrations,   .   .   . 93

CHAPTER VII.

SHADOW AND SUNSHINE.

War Record — Ph.D. — European Trip — His Daughter's
Death—The Silver Wedding, ... 112

CHAPTER VIII.

THE LAST DECADE.

Home Life—Somerville—Rothstein Lodge—A New Daughter—Correspondence—The Milton Shield—Signing his
Will, ... 129

CHAPTER IX.

A SAD SPRING-TIME.

The Last Birthday—Estimate of an Old Teacher—A Base
Attack—Offers his Resignation—Trustees Refuse to Accept—Letter from Professor Eaton—Death of Mrs. Crittenden—The Alumnæ Association,   .   .   . 149

CHAPTER X.

A GARNERED SHEAF.

PAGE

The Professor's Illness—Death in the Home—Last Visit to
Washington—Last Visit to the Packer—Fading Away—
The End—Journalistic Eulogiums—The Last Obsequies, . 168

APPENDIX.

I. Tributes to the Character of the late Professor CRIT-
TENDEN, ... 199
II. Funeral Addresses, ... 215
III. Extracts from Letters of Condolence, . . . 229
IV. Resolutions of Sympathy, ... 235

ALONZO CRITTENDEN.

CHAPTER I.

EARLY DAYS.

Parentage—Birth—Childhood—Education—College Life—Goes to
Albany—Mary Warner—Marriage—Offspring.

DAY after day the coffin-lid covers one and
another whose life-work, done well and
bravely, is accomplished, and the grave hides
forms and faces whose absence makes blanks in
domestic circles and solitude in human hearts; yet
society closes over the vortex with scarcely a rip-
ple to mark where the lives were lived. There
are others, however, who because of peculiar gifts
or graces, or it may be of the exceptional position
which they have occupied, have so struck the
roots of their individuality into the hearts and
homes of the community, that when they fall, a

great cry goes up and many are inclined to ask, " Who is left to take their places and to carry on their work?"

Such was the late Principal of the Packer Collegiate Institute and President of its Faculty of Instruction. A pioneer in the cause of the higher education of women, he entered upon his life-work at a period when to be a teacher of girls did not seem to promise either a brilliant or influential career. But he toiled on patiently, devoting to his work his best energies and his ripest judgment, subordinating to it private interests and social and domestic life; and his reward has been to live to see the enthusiasm of his early years placed in the foremost ranks of the onward progress of civilization. He has lived to see education for young women stand in the estimation of the community on the same plane with that provided for young men, and to have Wellesley and Vassar and Leroy and Cornell and the Harvard Annex attest what others following in his steps have done for our girls.

Dr. CRITTENDEN was a pioneer, and pioneers are not usually idealists, nor do they grasp their weapons with gloved hands and go forth into the wilderness delicately shod. They must take life as they find it, make the most of their appliances and their materials, and leave it for coming generations to do the finer work of polishing and adornment. "Those who try educators of 1825–1850 by standards of to-day will surely fail to appreciate the real service they rendered," says a correspondent.

The records of such a life should be preserved if only to afford to another time and generation an example of what persistent energy, spotless integrity, and consecrated devotion to one object can accomplish when joined to reverent and active Christian faith.

But such a life is difficult to chronicle, since its memorials exist partly in files of old and faded letters, and still more largely in the affectionate memories of those to whom its subject has been at once a father and a friend. Moreover it is by individual traits, or it may be by marked idiosyncrasies, that a man is distinguished from his fellows—his kindliness, his humor, his quickness at repartee, the trick of gesture, the sudden glance, the smile full of meaning—all of which are difficult if not impossible to reproduce.

The writer has done what she could do to present a life-like picture of the man with his sterling virtues and kindly traits, his distinctive peculiarities, and his loving, tender heart. Yet while appreciating the honor done her by those who have placed in her hands this " labor of love," she realizes ever more deeply her own inadequacy for its performance.

ALONZO CRITTENDEN, A.M., Ph.D., was born in the town of Richmond, Berkshire County, Massachusetts, April 7, 1801. He was the youngest but one of ten children, all of whom he outlived with the exception of an elder brother, Alvan, who, though for many years a great invalid, survived his distinguished brother by almost a year. One sister died young; all the other children reached the years of maturity.

Like most of the distinguished men of our age and country, the subject of this sketch was a self-made man. His father, Levi Crittenden, a substantial farmer, well known and highly respected in Berkshire County, came to Richmond when a young man, it is said as a mule-driver, from the South, though by birth he was a New-Englander. He was noted for his clear, cool judgment, and many incidents of his ready wit are traditional among the inhabitants. He is reported to have been a man of great physical strength, and the story is told of how one day when a neighbor was extremely abusive to him, he quietly picked the man up and dropped him over the fence. Another incident, showing the same intuitive perceptions joined to ready presence of mind which so distinguished the son of the Berkshire farmer, is thus told by his grandson :

" My grandfather, sitting at his front door one day, saw a man on horseback passing. Something in his manner caused the thought to occur to him that the man had stolen the horse on which he was riding. Going to the stable and saddling his own horse, he pursued. Looking back, and seeing he was being followed, the man whipped up. My grandfather whipped up. Soon both were on a dead run. My grandfather's horse was the faster. The man was brought back and locked

up, and the horse on which he had been riding
put in the stable. Some hours after, and while
my grandfather was reflecting, somewhat uneasily
perhaps, that he had arrested a man against whom
no charge had been made, without a warrant, and
on a mere suspicion for which he could scarcely
give a reason, some persons came up, and describing the man and the horse, asked if any one
answering to the description had been seen. To
their astonishment, my grandfather told them he
had both man and horse in custody. It turned
out that the man was a horse-thief."

Levi Crittenden married a lady of Guildford,
and took her at once to his newly-established
home in Richmond. Here his children were born,
and here they grew up surrounded by all the influences of the beautiful scenery of Berkshire
County, and here the temperate frugality and
comparative hardships of the farm-life of the period
developed in them manly independence and rugged strength. ·Better still, they were always surrounded by an atmosphere of the highest literary
culture, and in daily companionship with such
men as the Scargents, Primes, Fields, Sedgwicks,
and Wests.

Growing up thus among the rocks and hills of the Bay State, with a training that had in it no elements of effeminacy, the New England boy developed a tenacity of life which, in spite of his extremely delicate constitution, carried him safely beyond the fourscore years supposed to exceed the ordinary limit of human existence. To the same influences, perhaps, we may trace the sturdy independence which would not allow him to bur- den his father with the expense of a liberal educa- tion, which nevertheless, his ambition fired by the literary atmosphere he was constantly breathing, he resolved to have.

ALONZO attended the village school until he had learned all it could teach ; then, like so many other boys of the county, went to the Lenox Academy, where he made such good use of his time that he was prepared for college at sixteen. Proceeding at once to Schenectady, he entered Union Col- lege, then under the presidency of Dr. Eliphalet Nott, whose influence could be ever afterwards traced in his life and teachings.

The young collegian carried with him only fifty dollars of his father's money, a part of which he brought back at his first vacation, having by school teaching paid all his expenses and laid by enough money with which to commence the next term. He continued this practice throughout his college life,—which was by this drain upon his time necessarily protracted a little longer than is usual,—and never again cost his father any-thing.

Dr. CRITTENDEN's college course does not seem to have been especially marked by anything but faithfulness and energy; indeed, through life the successful and honored Principal was not so much distinguished for his scholarship as for other traits which go to build up beauty of character and to insure a high degree of success. He was, how-ever, admitted to the Phi Beta Kappa Society, an honorary distinction conferred only upon those whose scholarship is above the ordinary grade. Moreover, so good was his record, and so well had his supplementary career of teaching fitted him for the position, that at his graduation in 1824 he, a young man of only twenty-three years, was unanimously called to take part in the instruction of the Albany Female Academy, of which he soon after became Principal: a responsible position which he held for almost twenty years.

Of Mr. CRITTENDEN's social life in Albany very few records have been preserved. The family correspondence of that period has been almost totally destroyed; a few old pupils and teachers have kindly contributed their reminiscences, and an occasional remaining document preserved among the archives of the Albany Female Academy has been consulted and embodied in this work.

Dr. Charles E. West, himself an educator of ripe experience and deserved popularity, has in the article which the reader will find in the Appendix drawn a vivid picture of the "small community of brilliant and cultivated people" among whom Mr. CRITTENDEN began his life-work. In this community he was not only a welcome guest, but also a power. His popularity was great, and he numbered among his personal friends and intimates many of the really great men whose names are catalogued by Dr. West.

But alas! they have all passed away; their mute lips refuse to bear their testimony: he outlived his generation, and it is a second and a third which now rise to call him blessed.

The valuable correspondence which he must once have possessed has all perished, only a stray letter or two from old friends being found among his papers. One from his esteemed pastor, Rev. Dr. William B. Sprague, relates mainly to the marriage-ceremony which he performed for his young friend, thus uniting him with the noble woman who stood by his side for so many years as strengthener, counsellor, and friend; the wife whose well-being was ever his chief solicitude, and whose death left him for a few brief months in a loneliness which he said he never before imagined.

Dr. CRITTENDEN was a man who always held on to his friends, and the tie between him and his Albany pastor was one of peculiar strength and life-long endurance. It continued unbroken, in spite of changes of residence and pastoral relations, until the venerable doctor was called up higher some few years before his former parishioner.

Mr. CRITTENDEN's old pupils can doubtless recall how often he quoted Dr. Sprague's teachings and opinions. During the latter years of the old pastor's life he indulged in the harmless hobby of collecting autograph letters, poems, etc. Dr. CRITTENDEN interested himself in procuring these, and several of the later letters which have been preserved refer to this subject. The following is a specimen:

February 16, 1874.

MY DEAR MR. C.:

I know not what to say to you for your great kindness in procuring for me and sending to me so many invaluable autographs. I do thank you from the bottom of my heart, but that does not begin to do justice to my gratitude. I leave you to imagine the rest. . . .

I rejoice in all the prosperity of Packer Institute, as illustrating the clear vision of its illustrious Principal. I am yours most gratefully,

W. B. SPRAGUE.

If the mental and spiritual status of a man is, as some assert, to be measured by his reverence for his wife, ALONZO CRITTENDEN'S must be a high one. No sketch of him would be complete that did not give due importance to the life, personality, and influence upon him of Mary Wright

Warner. Miss Warner was born in Canaan, Columbia County, four miles from the early home of her husband, January 30, 1806. Her father was Elias Warner, whose venerable form and snowy hair were familiar to all the old pupils of the Brooklyn Female Academy, where he was book-keeper for several years; her mother died when her little girl was barely nine years old. She is represented by those who knew her in the early days when she first came to Albany as extremely beautiful. We who knew her in middle life and as age crept over her well remember the tall, stately figure, the dignified mien, the strong individuality of feature marked alike by kindliness and common-sense, and the blending of a certain homely sympathy which made her a person to be confided in while respected. So we Brooklyn girls felt about her, and so no doubt felt the Albany girls of an earlier day.

One of these writes:

" Miss Mary Warner comes up before me as a graceful, tall, dignified person, teaching me day by day, winning my early love. To her was written my first letter. How I wish I had her answer! Soon after, Miss Warner returned to Albany as Mrs. Crittenden."

Another old pupil says:

"I remember when I was a young girl how handsome she was, and I was afraid of her as I should have been of a queen or some one very far above me. Then when I was older, I felt it was the greatest favor that she would talk with me or treat me as a friend. I really loved her. She is associated with some of my earliest memories, when probably she did not know that small eyes and a small person were watching and admiring."

A letter of condolence written after her death by a former teacher in the Packer Institute thus speaks of this rare life-long companionship, as it appeared to a younger generation who knew Mrs. Crittenden in the later years of sorrow and pain which preceded her death:

"I feel almost as though my words should be those of congratulation, because of the beauty of the life so long your own, because of its rarely perfect accord with yours, because of the light from Heaven which illumined its entrance into the world which knows not pain nor death. It is a blessed thing to come to the earthly end of our closest ties with no need for one thought of self-reproach, no memory save one unbroken recollection of harmonious love. So I must needs count you rarely happy now, as in all these years you have been faithful and more than faithful to your first love. For you the past holds only sweetness, and the future only joy unspeakable."

Miss Mary Warner possessed a happy talent for versification, which she continued to exercise till the closing years of her life. Many of her pleasant little impromptus, written upon birthday occasions or in presenting and acknowledging gifts, still remain to attest the writer's talent and good feeling.

From among the little poems preserved in the family archives the following is selected, not so much because it is better than others, as because it exhibits that somewhat rare thing, the love of a husband and wife not cooled by the wear and tear of life, but as freshly beautiful and replete with sentiment as when two young hearts became one half a century before :

A BIRTHDAY TRIBUTE.

April 7, 1877.

Friend of my youth, and of my riper age,
Whose history blends with mine along life's page,
We've walked together through the rolling years,
Bearing each other's burdens, hopes, and fears.

Accept the thanks I ever owe to thee
For all thy faithful care and love to me ;
Forgive each word and every act of mine
That could have grieved a heart so true as thine.

  .   .   .   .

The shades of evening now begin to fall
Across the path that ends for us and all ;
May heavenly light, with ever-kindling ray,
Direct our course along the shadowy way !

And when the works of earth are fully done,
Our days all spent, our earthly courses run,
May faith assured look longingly above
To meet our Lord, the Lord of Life and Love !

YOUR AFFECTIONATE AULD WIFE.

Possibly this peculiar talent, prized at all times
by Mr. CRITTENDEN, first attracted his admiration
for the young poet; but her more substantial
qualities soon won his heart, and on August 5,
1829, the pair were married. Soon after they
opened the boarding-house for the Academy, over

which the young matron presided with such executive ability and graceful dignity for so many years, first in Albany and afterwards in Brooklyn.

Concerning Mr. CRITTENDEN's choice of a wife, Rev. Dr. Fulton in his funeral address says:

" Dr. CRITTENDEN believed in a womanly woman, not in a manly woman or a womanly man. He found a womanly woman in his wife. Because of this fact he trained women to be women; not women's rights women, nor women with missions especially, but women to beautify homes, to gladden life, and to carry out in life God's conception of woman when he placed her beside Adam in the garden of Eden. Mrs. Crittenden was cultured and fitted to adorn any circle, but she shone with most beautiful lustre in her home."

It was as " house-mother" that Mrs. Crittenden shone pre-eminently. Often at the head of a household of sixty or seventy, she was always equal to the occasion, never worried or flurried, doing with her might what her hands found to do. Watching with the sick, lending a sympathizing ear to troubles whose importance could only be measured by the suffering they inflicted; caring for her own little family, entertaining largely, doing her own share of church-work and taking her part in public charities, Mrs. Crittenden's life might advantageously bear the test of a comparison with Solomon's "virtuous woman."

Three children crowned this happy marriage : Catherine Seymour, born in Albany, May 16, 1830; Edward Warner, born in Albany, October 19, 1835; and Eliza Seymour, born after the family had removed to Brooklyn, in 1845.

On these children all the love of Mr. CRITTENDEN'S affectionate heart which was not absorbed by his wife was centred. Never was there a man of stronger family affections; he lived again in his children, and alas! suffered through them the deepest sorrows of his generally happy and successful life. But one of the three lives to mourn his loss; the others—the little one who, though dying almost in infancy, was to him ever a still-living reality, and the grown-up and accomplished daughter whose early death brought sorrow to so many hearts—both went before to welcome his home-coming at the last.

Of little Lilly he was wont to say, "When the

shepherd wants the sheep to follow, he carries the lambs in his bosom." The eldest daughter married Charles H. Dana of Brooklyn, lived long enough to present two little granddaughters to take, if possible, her place in her father's heart, and then faded away in her early womanhood at beautiful Mentone, on the Italian shore.

No doubt ere this he has met the three dear ones, mother and daughters, by the golden strand of that country ' where there shall be no more sea."

CHAPTER II.

THE ALBANY FEMALE ACADEMY.

Reminiscences of Old Scholars—Appreciation of the Trustees—
Professor Horsford's Memories—Dr. CRITTENDEN's Account—
Tribute of Pupils.

M R. CRITTENDEN'S history during the twenty years of his Albany life is largely that of the Academy at whose head he was placed. Its details have been difficult to gather, though multitudes of elderly women who remember their old instructor " in the kindness of their youth' speak with loving remembrances of his just severity tempered with kindness, and of the inspiration he gave to their lives.

One of these earlier pupils writes :

" I fear I cannot recall the daily life of over fifty years ago. While in Mr. CRITTENDEN's department I remember him as a young gentleman of pleasing manner, seeing all our foibles as it were at a glance, guiding us, making us feel the necessity of culture, genial, kind, truly desiring our best good. I remember his saying to me, 'Not a lazy thread in your body, only too full of mischief; you must apply yourself to study.' Once hearing a recitation in geography he said, 'Young ladies, go to your seats and study a half-hour.' I saucily replied, 'I know the lesson;' and I do believe, after making me sit down alone, he asked me about every question in it. He had made up his mind I should miss, and I did linger on the last question. However, I conquered; and his 'Well done' put us both in a good humor. We girls always thought nothing escaped his critical eye.

"I feel deeply grateful to Mr. CRITTENDEN for his implanting in my mind high aspirations. My youngest daughter was placed at the Packer; his greeting was always so pleasant, she learned to love him as I did."

A touching testimonial concerning those early school-days comes from a lady of over eighty years, who was one of the last visitors our venerable friend ever received, and whose acquaintance with him began in a remarkable way.

When a young woman, she married, and went

with her husband to reside on a large tract of land
in Canada, from which during some political con-
vulsions they were obliged to flee suddenly in the
night, leaving all their possessions behind them.
They reached Albany in a state of absolute destitution, and Mr. CRITTENDEN, who had known the
lady in her girlhood, at once gave her employ-
ment as teacher of the harp in his family, and so
provided for herself and her husband till the political storm had blown over and they were able
to return to their luxurious home.   She writes:

September 6, 1884.

DEAR MADAM:

   I have just received your letter, and it has caused
my soul to thrill with some of the dearest and sweet-
est memories of my friend Mr. CRITTENDEN, who still
lives in the hearts of thousands now ready to spring
forward and testify to the good which they have received from him, and to bequeath their own deep
love and reverence for him to their offspring.   .   .   .
For forty years I knew him, and in all that time
the beauty of his character with each passing de-
cade shone forth with a greater lustre, until he
reached the side of the blessed Master in whose service he had spent his life.   True, he had taught
worldly science; but he never forgot the spiritual.
He never forgot that Science and the great Book of
inspiration upon which our faith is founded can go

hand in hand and each dignify the other. This gave an irresistible force and charm to his teaching, and insured the happiest results. I had the honor and pleasure of possessing the friendship of this good man, together with that of his lovely family, and I esteemed it far beyond riches.

Yours very sincerely,
K. D.

The following letter comes from a life-long friend and pupil living in Montreal, who was wont till the close of her life to consult her old teacher in cases of perplexity and claim his sympathy in affliction and sorrow:

"It was my privilege to be placed under the care of the late Mrs. and Dr. CRITTENDEN at the age of fourteen, and during the four years I remained with them I experienced a loving care which endeared them to me for life. Dr. CRITTENDEN'S large sympathies and wonderful discernment of character gave him a magnetic influence over his pupils. The results of the labors of such a life can know no limit, they are as boundless as eternity. Thousands now living will ever remember with gratitude his loving, earnest, never-to-be-forgotten voice of counsel. His large heart

was always ready to cheer and comfort and pro-
tect the unfortunate and weak-hearted. His
hospitality knew no limit, and he had the happy
faculty of making a favor conferred felt to be a
favor received by him."

The pupils who boarded in Mr. CRITTENDEN's
family were, of course, better acquainted with
him than the day-scholars, and their reminiscences
of him are the fullest. Many of the Southern
girls remained with him during the vacations, and
to these he often stood in a relation of temporary
guardianship. Some of these retain very warm
recollections of their early friend. A lady in
Greenville, South Carolina, writes:

"In the years 1842 and '43 I was his pupil and
a member of his family. He impressed me as one
who was well furnished with the knowledge, the
characteristics of mind, the qualities of heart and
courtesies of life which made him the thorough
teacher, the true leader who pointed out the
wrong while he encouraged the right,—the tender
guardian, the kind friend with a ready sympathy
for those who were in trouble, and the true gentleman who honored woman in his intercourse with

his pupils. I can remember occasions, when embarrassed and excited, a word or look from him would put me entirely at ease. While he was just in administering reproof, words were never wasted, and when they had effected their purpose sunshine was at once restored; all was in the past, not to be brought forward again.

" I can only add my testimony to that of many others that the influence of those school-days was uplifting, encouraging, strengthening, and that ever after the name of Mr. CRITTENDEN was mentioned with reverence and love.

" For many years we had no personal intercourse, and our lives seemed to drift apart, until circumstances brought us together again in the year 1870. Then it was as though we had never parted, for there was the same bright, cheerful spirit, the same quick, elastic movement which made us recognize him in his playful assumed disguise, and we found, my sister and myself, the same true heart which having once professed friendship changes not, his own words expressing it concisely —' once, now, and forever your friend.' "

That Mr. CRITTENDEN'S own generous kindness had a great deal to do with cementing lasting bonds of affectionate respect not only with his pupils but also with their parents, the following letter found among his papers will prove:

May 9, 1845.

My Dear Sir:

In reference to the very kind treatment my children have received, I must just repeat here what I have already said in my previous letter. I feel that I really want terms to express the accumulated obligations under which your kind sister and yourself have laid me for the truly unmeasured acts of goodness experienced from you by my children, and that certainly in very trying circumstances, that were as little anticipated by me, when last in Albany, as was the great extent of these kind and generous acts which they occasioned.

I can only now add that I must in the first place endeavor my best to discharge the more nominal part of the debt that comes under the denomination of dollars and cents as soon as possible, and then plead bankruptcy for the weightier part which makes claims on my gratitude that I am unable to meet. . . .

A. A. T.

The gentlemen who had placed Mr. CRITTEN DEN at the head of their institution seem to have held him in high esteem; and that this esteem was much prized by him is evident from the care with which the yellow paper containing the following resolutions has through all these years been treasured.

From the scanty records of the time it appears that a certain teacher had brought grave charges against the Principal concerning which he indignantly demanded a full investigation; this document and the action it embodied were probably the result of this investigation.

RESOLUTION PASSED BY THE BOARD OF TRUSTEES OF THE ALBANY FEMALE ACADEMY, AUGUST 4, 1829.

Resolved, unanimously, That the Treasurer pay to the Principal of the Academy the sum of one hundred dollars, as a special mark of the respect and esteem which this Board entertain for him, and of their confidence in his ability and fidelity.

W. BOYD, *Chairman.*
GIDEON HAWLEY, *Secretary.*

Professor E. N. Horsford now of Cambridge, Mass., was for several years Mr. CRITTENDEN's Assistant and Professor of Natural Sciences and Mathematics in the Albany Academy. A very warm friendship grew up between the two co-laborers, which never cooled as the years went by ; indeed a constant repetition of mutual good offices only made it grow stronger to the end.

The present ill-health of the Professor makes it impossible for him to contribute the full account of the Albany Academy and its Principal which was solicited for this memorial. In a brief note of apology he says :

" I fear there is nothing of Mr. CRITTENDEN'S in print that will aid you.

" He taught two books only,—the same that Dr. Nott taught at Union College,—Kames' ' Elements of Criticism ' and Butler's ' Analogy.' He brought with him from Union College, where he graduated, all Dr. Nott's choice anecdotes in illustration of these two books.

" The grading of the Academy at Albany arose I do not know how. It was twenty years before I became a teacher there. It was essentially the same as that of the Packer Collegiate Institute. At Albany the great achievement was composition. I do not think the study of Latin and Greek was pursued. There was French. But the stress was laid upon composition as the expression of the study of English. For public exhibition there was nothing like the classes in Kames and Butler. The young ladies talked and wrote wonderfully well.

" I do not think Mr. CRITTENDEN had any idea of young ladies pursuing studies in the same plane with college students. I think his general idea— and in this I think he pursued much the same course that Mrs. Willard did—was that ladies should be fitted specially to preside over households ; and to this end the great accomplishments were talking upon the great topics in taste, mental and moral philosophy, criticism and analysis, and *writing.*"

Another teacher of those days says :

" Our old Principal was ever a man of supreme devotion to the duty of the hour ; he never wasted strength on side issues, nor diluted the influence his strong individuality brought to bear upon the business in which he was engaged by spreading it over a variety of enterprises at once. Indeed the secret of his success through life, and that by which he made three successive educational institutions successful, was his personal adoption of that rule of Lord Brougham's which he so con

stantly urged upon his pupils—' Be the whole
man at one thing at a time.' "

Dr. West, who of all men living knew most
about the Academy, its inception and its history,
has told the whole with great succinctness in his
"letter" (published in the Appendix), and his work
need not be duplicated.

Mr. CRITTENDEN was always a man of action,
and he has left few written records of his opinions
on educational or other cognate topics. On one
occasion, being called upon to furnish some con-
tribution for the educational department of a
work to be entitled " The Public Service of the
State of New York," he dictated a paper which, as
it describes the whole movement which resulted
in the successive founding of the Albany Female
Academy, the Brooklyn Female Academy, and
the Packer Collegiate Institute, is in place at this
point. Some extracts at least will be of interest
to the reader. The work has since been completed at great expense, and sent to all the leading
libraries of Europe.

THE PACKER INSTITUTE.

This institution sustains the closest relation, if indeed it may not be almost considered as identical, with the very earliest endowment for purposes of female education in the State of New York. In the year 1811, Chancellor Kent, John V. Henry, Gideon Hawley, and others, of like purpose and culture, residing in Albany, desiring facilities for the higher education of their daughters, formed an association, erected buildings, provided a library, apparatus, etc., and commenced operations.

The institution increased, and soon required more ample accommodations. In 1821 the association was incorporated by the Legislature under the name and title of the Albany Female Academy. The Legislature, at the same time, donated one thousand dollars to the institution, the first money ever appropriated by the State of New York for female education.

The late Chancellor Ferris was for several years President of the Board of Trustees, and after his removal to the city of New York exerted his influence in founding the Rutgers Female Institute—now Rutgers College.

In 1844 an institution intended to be modelled on the same general plan was established in this city under the name of the Brooklyn Female Academy, and was incorporated the same year by the State Legislature.

It is believed that the principal female institutions of this and other States for the higher education of women, in a very great degree, had their origin in the thought and enterprise of Chancellor Kent, and his associates, in the early part of the century. .

Recognizing the constantly increasing claims of cultured society, the Faculty of the Packer Institute have sought not so much to emulate the fame of universities, as to prepare their pupils for the actual duties and responsibilities that await them. Learning is made subservient to life. The methods of instruction are based upon the "drawing-out process" rather than the "pouring-in process." The great effort of the teachers is to help the student to help herself. Personal assistance in study is only given when the problem is evidently beyond the powers of the pupil.

In February, 1843, the Trustees of the Albany Academy, in presenting their semi annual report, bore this testimony to their appreciation of the character and services of the Principal, who had been again maligned by some malicious enemies:

"The Trustees regret that the recent attempt to injure the Academy by anonymous publications and more private insinuations and slanders should render it expedient to add anything to what has been already said. But as faithful guardians of the interests committed to their trust, they deem it proper to say both to the stockholders and the public that they are not aware of any just ground for the attacks which have been made upon the institution or the individuals connected with it.

To meet an unfortunate reduction in the amount of income, all our expenditures have been reduced so far as that could be done without impairing the high character and usefulness of the institution. The Principal, without abating anything of his zeal to maintain the reputation of the school, has for the last two years voluntarily relinquished five hundred dollars of his salary.

.   .   .   .   .

"It is due to the Principal of the Academy to say that he has labored for nineteen years with eminent success in the station which he occupies, and that he enjoys the unabated confidence of every member of the Board."

To this testimonial, the last which this Board ever had an opportunity of offering to their Principal, are appended the names of the Trustees:

THE ALBANY FEMALE ACADEMY.

Another pleasant tribute of affection and esteem which reached the Principal about this time—the close of his services in Albany—was a New Year's gift from sixty-six of his pupils, whose names were appended to the following note:

Will Mr. CRITTENDEN kindly accept from the young ladies of the Academy the accompanying set of chess, as an expression of their affectionate regard for his untiring exertions not only for their intellectual attainments, but for the cultivation of their moral sentiments without which all other acquirements are useless? They sincerely wish him a Happy New Year, and desire each successive one may return him a richer harvest of love and gratitude.

HANNAH J. SKINNER,
ELOISE A. HUNTING,
                Committee.

ALBANY, January 1, 1843.

CHAPTER III.

THE BROOKLYN FEMALE ACADEMY.

Call for Meeting of Citizens—Invitation to Dr. CRITTENDEN—
Letter of Acceptance—Move to Brooklyn—Professor Alonzo
Gray—Academy Built—Opening—The Principal—The Library
—Anecdotes.

AS stated both by Dr. CRITTENDEN and Dr.
West* several distinguished Brooklyn gentlemen were, as early as 1840, desirous of establishing in their city a girls' school similar in
character and design to the Albany Female Academy and Rutgers Institute in New York. A
brief sketch of the inception, preliminary arrangements, and final carrying out of this plan may be
gathered from the minutes of the early Trustees'
meetings, still preserved in the archives of the
Packer Institute.

The following call was issued December 19,
1844:

* See Appendix.

Female Education.

A meeting of the friends of Female Education in this city will be held in the Hamilton Room in the Brooklyn Institute (late Lyceum), on Friday evening next, the 20th inst., at 7 o'clock, to adopt suitable measures for the establishment of a Young Ladies' Institute, upon a plan similar to the Rutgers Female Institute in the city of New York.

It is expected that the Rev. Dr. Ferris, President of the Rutgers Institute, and other gentlemen, will address the meeting.

The signatures of twelve leading citizens were appended, and in answer to the call a large, enthusiastic gathering of those favorable to the cause was held on the appointed evening; George Wood, Esq., presiding, and Francis Spies acting as secretary.

After some very interesting remarks delivered by the Rev. Dr. Ferris, President of Rutgers Female Institute, on the subject of female education, a committee of five was appointed to open a subscription for the capital stock of a higher school for girls and make application for a charter for the same at the ensuing legislature. Messrs. A. Crist, M. Kimball, W. S. Packer,

Francis Spies, and D. G. Cartwright composed the committee.

Another meeting was held in the room of the Common Council, January 11, 1845, with Cyrus P. Smith in the chair. Dr. Ferris made a second address, after which the chairman of the committee reported that a fund of thirty thousand dollars would be needed to carry out the proposed enterprise, of which twenty-four thousand dollars had already been obtained. The first Board of Trustees was then elected. Their names were as follows:

George Wood,	Thomas Baylis,
E. D. Hurlburt,	John H. Prentice,
W. S. Packer,	John Skillman,
Seth Low,	J. H. Smith,
Abraham Crist,	D. G. Cartwright,
Francis Spies,	W. I. Cornell,
Peter Clark,	O. H. Gordon,

David Coope.

These names, "familiar in our ears as household words" in the days when we were "Academy girls," are, all but one, now names of the dead. But their owners laid broad foundations, and builded wisely thereon for future generations.

They rest from their labors, but their works do follow them. The womanhood of the nation owes them its suffrages. Perchance they have already welcomed home him whom they first welcomed to the headship of their infant institution and who outlived them all but one.

There was some hesitation as to the name of the new school, the choice balancing for some time between the "Nassau Female Academy" and the "Brooklyn Female Academy"—the latter being adopted March 15th. On the 4th of that month the site of the building—the same as that now occupied by the Packer Collegiate Institute —was decided upon, after considerable objection on the ground that "it was too far away from the thickly populated portion of the city"!

On May 17, 1845, the Instruction Committee unanimously recommended to the Trustees to invite Mr. ALONZO CRITTENDEN of Albany to accept the appointment of Principal of the Brooklyn Female Academy, at a salary of two thousand dollars. Mr. Seth Low moved the adoption of the recommendation.

Mr. CRITTENDEN sent this letter of acceptance :

ALBANY FEMALE ACADEMY,
June 6, 1845.

John H. Prentice, Esq.

MY DEAR SIR: Will you have the goodness to communicate to your associates of the Committee and to the Board of Trustees you represent my acceptance of the invitation tendered to me in your letter of the 19th instant to take the charge as Principal of the Brooklyn Female Academy?

The decision I now announce is one deeply affecting my future usefulness and happiness, and it has been made under circumstances of so much embarrassment that an earlier reply has been impracticable. For the generous indulgence granted for the consideration of this important subject you will please accept my thanks.

If I have not misapprehended your Committee, you will expect my service for the first of September. In the mean time it will be my interest and happiness at any and all times to co-operate with your Trustees or any of their committees in any efforts to promote the interest of your institution.

I cannot doubt but with the enlarged views entertained by your Board of Trustees and the liberal facilities proposed to be furnished that the Brooklyn Female Academy will at no distant time take rank with the first-class seminaries in the country, and be an ornament and pride to your beautiful city.

For yourself and each member of your Board accept my best wishes for your health and happiness.

Most truly and respectfully
Your obedient servant,
A. CRITTENDEN.

In accordance with this letter Mr. CRITTENDEN moved to Brooklyn with his family as soon after the close of the Albany term as he could make it convenient to do so, and at once devoted himself to superintending the building arrangements and laying plans for the future prosperity of the new academy.

On the 25th of November Professor Alonzo Gray was engaged, at a salary of twelve hundred dollars, and at once entered upon the work of superintending the laboratory, apparatus, etc.

So efficient did this joint supervision prove, and so rapidly was the work pressed forward, that the new academy building was opened for inspection on Monday, May 5, 1846. Public exercises were held in the chapel the same evening, at 7.30 P.M., on which occasion the address was made by the Principal's old pastor, Dr. Wm. B. Sprague, of Albany. His new pastor, Dr. I. S. Spencer, was also present, and took, then as ever after till his greatly lamented death, a warm interest in the institution and its concerns. The next week, May 14, 1846, the school was opened with three hundred and fifty pupils.

The first term was necessarily experimental; plans were to be tried, departments graded, the curriculum adjusted, and the brief weeks of late spring and early summer proved all too short for the work. No class was graduated that year.

One of Dr. CRITTENDEN'S most marked traits was his keen insight into character. His rare wisdom in the selection of his teachers was one of the potent agencies by which he secured the success of his schools. The first Board of Instruction was largely made up of Albany material, both teachers and older scholars. They knew him, understood his methods and idiosyncrasies, and thus the whole Board worked together in harmony from the start. Mr. CRITTENDEN was not only Principal of the Academy; he was its *overseer* in the fullest sense of that word. Nothing that occurred in the great building, from garret to cellar, escaped his supervision. The pupils considered him ubiquitous: so quiet was his light, elastic footstep, and so great the agility with which he was wont to dart from one story to another in search of possible disorder or need of discipline, that the girls never knew whether he was looking at them or not.   He personally exemplified the truth of another favorite motto: "The eye of the master can do more work than both his hands."   Every teacher who has ever taught under his supervision cannot but remember how constantly he quoted for their benefit a well-known aphorism slightly altered to suit the circumstances: "' Eternal vigilance is the price of' other things besides ' liberty.' "

The first class which was graduated from the Brooklyn Female Academy, July 21, 1847, consisted of thirteen members whose faded signatures are still appended to the following graceful little poem of

FAREWELL.

Pleasant, oh ! very pleasant to our tread
Hath been this path in which for a brief while
Thy hand hath led us,—thou whom our young hearts
Revere and love ; thou who hast been to us
A kindly teacher, counsellor and friend.
Yet tears are gathering in our eyes this hour,
Warm tears and sad, to think that all so soon
We in thine ear must breathe a sad "Good-by."

Oft will our hearts turn to these classic halls,
Oft of thy welfare ask, and often breathe
An earnest prayer that God may be with thee ;
May be with all who to thy care are given !

Years, weary years may pass ere we shall reach
The home our Father God hath promised us ;
Yet ne'er may we forget thy words, our friend ;
Ne'er cease to ask that in that better home
We on thy face once more may gladly look !
And now farewell ! farewell !   May the slight gift
We place with grateful hearts within thy hand
Be a memento of the pleasant hours
That under thy kind guidance we have passed !

The preservation for so many years of this little
time-worn waif, when the correspondence of the
great and the good has nearly all perished, shows
the warm appreciation of the kind recipient for
the girlish love which dictated it.

An old pupil, afterwards a teacher and now a
writer for the press, says:

"It was in the autumn of 1847 that I first became acquainted with Dr. CRITTENDEN, and
commenced a friendship, fatherly on his side,
and on mine full of grateful affection, which
nothing could ever shake or weaken.   I well remember how, a little shivering child, I was taken
to the Academy and consigned to its Principal ;
how, utterly unused to contact with others, and
prepared for school life only by desultory home
study, I 'lingered trembling at the brink, and

feared to launch away,' till he kindly won from me
what I did know, and placed me just where de-
ficiencies could be rectified without sensitiveness
being mortified. I remember, moreover, how
quick he was to recognize from the first the
facilis scribendi, and by even more than judicious
commendation to encourage the taste that might
perhaps have lain buried under other things, thus
paving the way towards the attainment of honorable competence, and preparing a consecrated pen
to attempt some little service in the Master's
cause.

"Another reminiscence of those early days is
the Commencement night, when, as the hour for
leave-taking came, I sobbed, in girlish fashion, ' I
wish *you* were my father; then I should not have
to go away.' And his response was, 'Never
mind; I will be your second father and friend
always.'

"Most faithfully was that promise kept. As
life's duties and responsibilities thickened, his was
the counsel always sought, the advice generally
taken; and when in a few years it became necessary to seek a position of usefulness and emolu-

ment, his interest secured one in the dear Alma
Mater.   Here for a long succession of years I
was in almost daily intercourse with him, and
learned to appreciate the good points in his
rather unique character."

Prominent among these points was executive
ability, the power of governing without seeming
to control, of dissolving complications without
open ruptures, of divining as by intuition the
persons and measures most conducive to the
inherent excellence, as well as the outward reputation, of the institution; and no doubt its unexampled prosperity and continued success were
largely due to this peculiar combination of qualities.

The recitation-hours devoted to the studies then
taught by Mr. CRITTENDEN—Kames' Elements—
Butler's Analogy, Abercrombie's Intellectual Philosophy, Paley's Natural Theology, and Wayland's
Moral Science—were looked forward to by some
of his pupils with anticipations of unmixed delight.   His repetition of Dr. Nott's anecdotes,—
all new to them,—with multitudes of fresh illustrations and witty sayings of his own, were a

constant source of interest ; while the simple way
he had of incidentally introducing sacred themes,
not perfunctorily, but as though they were the
most natural outgrowth of the subject, was exceedingly impressive.

"Whatever may be the experience of others,"
writes the pupil before quoted, "I always feel
that my first religious impressions were the result
of those words. Reverence for the Bible, belief
in orthodoxy, and a personal sense of responsibility seemed to grow and thrive in the atmosphere of those daily *séances.* Even now, after an
interval of over thirty years, memory reconstructs
the picture of that beloved library, the walls lined
with glass cases containing books, birds, and curi-
osities. In the centre stands a long table with a
group of eager, bright-eyed girls (mostly gray-
headed now) seated around it. At the head sits
the Principal, looking, with his dark brown, silky
curls and slight, elastic figure, altogether too
young to be father to a girl older than any of
these, and with him usually some kindly minister
or literary man, ready to puzzle us with hard
questions, or, as we thought in our youthful van-

ity, to admire our proficiency and fluency in recitation."

Prominent among these remembered great ones
are Dr. Samuel Hanson Cox, full of word-puzzles
and the wonderful properties of language; Dr. S. I.
Prime, then as ever a keen *observer;* Dr. Spencer,
kind, fatherly, and considerate; Henry Ward
Beecher, young, enthusiastic, and always in a
hurry; Dr. Lewis, of Trinity, grave and preoccu-
pied; Dr. William S. Stone, of Christ Church; Dr.
Gallaudet, pioneer in the instruction of the deaf
and dumb; Dr. Backus, Dr. Bethune, Dr. Rock-
well, and many more the fame of whose names
is in all the churches and abroad in the land.

Many other reminiscences of those recitation-
hours are still extant. No man ever knew so well
how to handle a class for exhibition; how to
bring out the real information of timid scholars,
and to give the reins to the fluent ones. But
should there chance to be no company present, the
shirks who had hoped to escape under cover of
the good scholars always came to grief. The
teacher would hold the text-book open before
him and say quietly,

" Next young lady. Next topic."

Not a word of question or suggestion would follow; and after an appalling silence he would say,

"Can't you say *something*, or *do* something? Throw an inkstand at me, like Luther, if you can do no more. Let me see that you are alive."

At the head of this library-table sat the Principal at all hours of the day, when not engaged in flitting about the building—a terror to evil-doers, a voice of praise to them that did well. And here the girls often brought him their private perplexities and puzzles, receiving from his ready sympathy help, instruction, disentanglement, as the case might demand. There were girls who held that library-table in holy awe, but they did not, as a rule, belong to Mr. CRITTENDEN'S own classes.

The Brooklyn Female Academy only existed eight years, and its memorials are even more difficult to find than those connected with the Albany school. They are treasured in the hearts and memories of many of the mothers and grandmothers of the land who are still in the thick of the battle of life, and have little time or opportunity to sit down and write the things they might be very ready to say.

During those eight years the school was growing in usefulness, and the character of its Principal was developing and strengthening amid the labors and under the discipline of life.

Many incidents of these days, illustrative of traits of character, are remembered by Mr. CRITTENDEN'S friends. The following has been kindly furnished:

One night Mrs. Crittenden was suddenly awakened by the light of a candle, and thinking some one might be sick in the house, called out the name of the cousin who lived with the family and aided in the housekeeping, supposing that she had come down for medicine or something.

Receiving no reply, she got up, went out of her bedroom, heard footsteps and followed them to the head of the basement stairs. There she felt a draught of air, and the idea of burglars flashed into her mind. Returning to the bedroom, she felt for her watch, and not finding it, she awoke her husband and told him that burglars were in the house.

"Nonsense!" he said; but reaching for his watch and not finding it, continued: "Call Thomas." Thomas was a waiter, a raw Irishman who did not know enough to be afraid of anything.

When Thomas appeared, Mr. CRITTENDEN told him to go to Fulton Ferry and arrest any person that might be there, while he would go to the South Ferry and do the same thing. There were only two Brooklyn ferries then, and Mr. CRITTENDEN'S theory was that all evil-doers came from New York.

On his way to the ferry Mr. CRITTENDEN stopped at the mayor's house. The mayor put his head and night-cap out of the window.

"Burglars have been in my house. What shall I do?"

"Go home and go to bed."

"I mean to catch the rascals."

"That's a good joke." And the mayor took his own advice and went to bed.

On his way to Fulton Ferry Thomas met a watchman who offered to go with him. At the

ferry, the ticket-agent said that two men had just
gone on board of the boat. Thomas went on the
boat and saw the two men, one of whom had a
bundle. He returned, reported to the watchman,
and both of them went on the boat, and, though
neither of the two men there had a bundle, they
took the responsibility of arresting both.

Early the next morning Mr. CRITTENDEN in-
duced the ferry company to run their boats into
another slip, and offered a reward for anything
stolen from his house that might be fished up
from the bottom of the East River. A dozen or
more boats, with hooks or rakes, were soon trolling about the pier. In less than twenty minutes
the stolen watches were fished up.

Some other things were found, and the rob-
bers were sent to State prison for fifteen years.

Mr. CRITTENDEN'S son loves to tell this story,
while exhibiting the identical watch, in illustration of his father's readiness in emergencies, his
promptness in action, quick decision, fertility in
resources, persistence in resolution, and complete
success in whatever he undertook.

The watch must have been of wonderful workmanship, for its salt bath does not appear to have hurt it at all; and many a delinquent of after years, in the morning or at " recess," anxious to utilize the last moment for play or gossip, is familiar with its face, held up with an air of good-humored threatening and admonition.

CHAPTER IV.

LAST DAYS OF THE ACADEMY.

Discipline—An Old Teacher—Religious Influence—Dr. Spencer—
Sorrows—A Change of Professors—The Fire.

MR. CRITTENDEN'S ideas of discipline, commenced in the early days of the Brooklyn Female Academy and adhered to till the end in the government of the Packer Institute, never varied. One who was constantly with him in the office and had many opportunities of knowing and understanding him writes:

" He was always careful not to allow a girl to be disgraced if it were possible to avoid it. Even when she had committed a serious fault he trusted to the reformatory power of self-respect, and feared to drive her to a loss of this quality by making her feel that others did not respect her and that the best things were not expected of her. This was not a mere theory of his, but a principle of conduct which I never knew him to violate."

The same close observer, to whom was for many years entrusted the copying and custody of the minutes of the Trustees' meetings, further says:

"During the first year or two of the Brooklyn Female Academy cases of discipline among the girls were occasionally acted upon by the Board of Trustees. Later, and ever since, nothing of that character came up for official action. Mr. CRITTENDEN settled all such matters and all disagreements with teachers. He used to say: 'I am captain of this ship. Providence has indicated the necessity of one head to every animal.' I do not think that this was any assumption of authority upon his part, or any jealousy of outside or official interference. He showed his worldly wisdom by dealing with such matters quietly; knowing how much bad blood is stirred by publicity, and how the original grievance may become as nothing compared with the bitterness of partisanship which public disputes engender."

A lady for many years the wife of a distinguished Brooklyn physician, but in her youth a teacher in the Brooklyn Female Academy, has

furnished for this memorial the following delightful reminiscences:

"As to Dr. CRITTENDEN, I wish I could help
you more than I can. I have nothing of the letter
kind to give. I have had letters from him, but I
seldom preserve letters, and think I have destroyed all of his. They were generally short and
on business matters. I do not believe Mr. CRIT-
TENDEN was much of a letter-writer. He was too
nervous a man to confine himself in that way. I
think his great strength lay in his quickness; details were a bore to him. I have thought his
great executive ability lay most in the suddenness
of his action; he was ubiquitous. Wasn't it wonderful how he governed that school with no rules?
'Do right' included it all. I don't believe such a
case was ever known before. He read human
nature very easily, and knew how to take advantage of the fact.

"I think of Mr. CRITTENDEN as one of the most
kindly, warm-hearted men I ever knew; most sympathetic and generous. He was not understood by
many. He did a world of good that never came to
the light; his purse was always open for suffering.

I recall this example: My father, in one of his missionary tours, found a family in great destitution, without food or fuel, in one of our coldest winter days and in a raging snow-storm. They had come from the West Indies; had pawned nearly all their clothing and other necessaries in New York. My father came home and told the story. I went to school with my sympathies all aroused for these poor people, and meeting Mr. CRITTENDEN, told it to him. Without a moment's hesitation he asked if my father could get the pawn-tickets. I went home and got them, and he set out in that fearful storm and was nearly all the day redeeming those tickets, besides whice he sent money to the family, and never a word said about it.

"Do you remember H—— C—— who came to the Institute? She was very bright and very determined to have an education, but she was entirely dependent. I became quite interested in her and took her into our family. She couldn't dress decently, and she felt it. "One day Mr. CRITTENDEN came to me and said it troubled him to see her not dressed as well as the others. I told him that she had no money even to pay board; that she couldn't go to church for want of clothes. He at once handed me a well-filled purse and said, 'Take all you need for her. I want her to feel she can do as others do; get her a good dress,' etc.

"I often went to him for her afterward, and he was always ready to help.

"When she left school and had graduated with honor, she said to Mr. CRITTENDEN that she hoped to pay him. He told her that if she was ever able she might, but the next world would do as well."

Another friend calls to remembrance Mr. CRITTENDEN'S unerring intuitions concerning the way to deal with each scholar who needed discipline. He had no general rules; each case was managed by itself, and usually with great success. The following, communicated by a pupil of later years, is a case in point:

"The wonderful degree of harmony which for so many years existed among so many hundreds of teachers and pupils was perhaps directly trace-able to him. His tact in the management of those under his control was wonderful. As a disciplinarian he had few equals. An incident which shows superlative delicacy in dealing with what seemed difficult cases he once related to me as follows:

"A young girl from the South who was a pupil at the Institute was continually in disgrace and frequently reported to him by her teachers. One day calling her to him in his kind, fatherly way, and without charging her with the slightest fault, he said, 'I do not think, my child, that this is the place for you. You do not seem happy here, and I would be very sorry to have you stay and lose your time. I do not think you are gaining as you should, and it will be better for you to go to some other place.' She burst into tears and said, 'May I try again?' 'Nothing would please me better, if you wish it,' he replied.

"She *did* try, and no further complaint was heard. She became a diligent and happy student.

"In his social life with the students he was exceedingly agreeable. He was quick at re-partee, and very happy and ready in his choice of anecdotes, of which he told many."

Mr. CRITTENDEN was eminently a peace-maker;

" a soft answer" always turned away his wrath, even when his severity was just ; indeed it may be said that a saucy one often did the same, provided it was bright and witty and not tinctured with pertness or insubordination.

The general religious tone of the school in those days was good, especially among the boarders. Dr. Spencer watched over them as one who must give account for souls, and many a young woman who came from a distant home, in order to acquire treasures of earthly wisdom carried back with her something of still greater value, even the pearl of great price. Many of Dr. Spencer's well-known " Pastor's Sketches" are drawn from his recollections and notes of the conversion of these young girls. Mr. CRITTENDEN and his pastor were in perfect accord, and there existed between them a beautiful and tender friendship, commenced during college days, suspended—not broken—by the untimely death of the minister in the flower of his usefulness, November 23, 1854.

One of Dr. Spencer's daughters says of her old teacher and friend : " You know our intimacy was not exactly like that of teacher and scholar. I can only say that as a friend he was ever kind and sympathetic. To both himself and his wife I could go, and did go, whenever I needed a cheering word. Those words came with peculiar kindness from Mr. CRITTENDEN, and great wisdom in advice. He gave to the child what he had received from the father, guidance in perplexity. He was with us in that dark hour when our father passed away from earth. The scene is just as vivid to-day as then, and his own tender grief was never forgotten by us children."

Dr. CRITTENDEN was always extremely particular that every member of the school should be present at the prayer-service with which every session was opened. No excuse for absence was accepted; it was with the greatest difficulty that pupils resident in suburban towns or a neighboring State and dependent upon public conveyances could be considered "permanently excused" in such a way as not to lower their standing in scholarship or deportment. Even teachers of specialties, whose duties did not call them to the Institute till the middle of the forenoon, often found themselves in the dilemma of losing either time valuable to them in other directions or the good opinion of the Principal.

Some of us who in past days considered the stress laid upon this point as bordering upon the unreasonable now look back upon it as an earnest testimony in favor of religion and a practical comment upon the text, " In *all* thy ways acknowledge Him" of inestimable value in the moulding of our lives. Equally strict was our Principal in enforcing proper decorum and appropriate reverence during this solemn service; often have we heard him say with a look which said more than the words, " Young ladies, 'even the angels veil their faces;' shall poor miserable mortals come into the divine presence with fool's eyes directed to the ends of the earth?"

The Book of Proverbs, by the bye, was ever his favorite choice for our morning lesson, and the emphasis with which he would read, " Wisdom is the principal thing; therefore *get* wisdom," will be remembered by many who read these pages.

The first severe personal discipline of his life came during these years, in the loss of his little Lilly, born after the removal to Brooklyn, and taken into the upper nursery when about eighteen months old. All the tenderness of her father's peculiarly affectionate nature was touched by this bereavement, and never to the day of his death could he speak of this little one without a tear in his voice. This chastening so affected him as to make him a blessed comforter to those afflicted like himself, as the family of the writer soon afterwards experienced, when on the last day of 1851 its household pet was taken away.

Another serious disappointment awaited him in the sudden failure of the health of his eldest daughter, which prevented her completing the severe course of study necessary for graduation, and sent her to the Brattleboro Water Cure at the time when her class received their diplomas.

Mr. CRITTENDEN seems to have been generally popular both inside and outside of the school· Mistakes he may have sometimes made, and detraction can never be entirely escaped by any one in a public position ; but the sole official record of the time, the Trustees' minutes, bear no traces of them.

In 1852 Professor Gray left the Academy and opened a school of his own, the Brooklyn Heights

Seminary, now in the hands of Dr. Charles E. West. The vacancy thus made in the Faculty was filled by the appointment of Darwin G. Eaton, who holds a place in the affections of all the teachers and pupils only second to that of the beloved Principal himself.

Not a jar or a mist of disagreement ever came between these two destined to be united for so large a portion of their lives; both strangely called to lay down their work and unbuckle their armor almost at the same moment. As unlike as it is possible to imagine two men, they walked thenceforth arm in arm through life; and only a few weeks ago the Professor said to the writer,

" Never did I have a friend like him; with all his peculiarities, he was to me a brother; yes, much more than a brother."

But the days of the Brooklyn Female Academy, so carefully planned, so successfully carried on, such a benediction to the city, so full of promise for the future, were numbered. The school closed the day before Christmas for the usual midwinter vacation in perfect order and flourishing condition; but just as the scholars were looking for-

ward to reassembling, after the holidays, at eight
o'clock on the morning of New Year's Day, 1853,
tongues of flame were seen shooting from crevices,
clouds of smoke curled out of windows, and in a
few hours the commodious building, with all its
furniture, library, laboratory, etc., was a heap
of smouldering ashes, while from multitudes of
homes throughout the city went up a pathetic
wail of sorrow for the lost Alma Mater.

But no time was wasted in useless wailing by
either Principal or Trustees. Before the fires
were fairly subdued, at one o'clock on that event-
ful New Year's Day, which happened to be Saturday, a meeting of the Board was held at the Brooklyn Institute (Lyceum) in Washington Street, " to
take such action as might be deemed most conducive to the future interests of the Institution."
At this meeting the Finance Committee was em-
powered to engage rooms for the temporary ac-
commodation of the school in the Brooklyn Institute. At the same time the Principal, knowing
that the occupancy of these could be but temporary, was, with his usual indomitable energy, making arrangements for hiring and furnishing two

large old mansions, well known to Brooklyn citizens, farther up the same street.

Thus not a moment was lost. On Monday
morning, at the usual school hour, the shepherd
gathered his shelterless flock around him, conducted prayers in the Lyceum hall, dispersed the
classes as well as he could through the building,
and saw that the regular recitations were all in
progress. Never did his perfect power of con-
trolling others show itself so pre-eminently as
during those three or four days during which several hundred restless and excitable young girls
were kept in order and taught in circumstances
so conducive to the relaxation and destruction of
all proper discipline.

Before the week closed one of the old houses was
ready for occupation, and in a short time the other,
connected with it by a temporary covered gallery,
received those pupils who still assembled at the
Lyceum, and here the Brooklyn Female Academy
spent the last year of its brief life. The attendance of course fell off somewhat, as indeed there
was not room for so many pupils; but the prosperity was unabated, and in July a fine class was

graduated at the Brooklyn Athenæum, where the Commencement exercises were held.

The last meeting of the Trustees of the Brooklyn Female Academy was held February 27, 1854, at which time the following resolution was passed :

Resolved, That a final dividend of one hundred and fifty-eight $\frac{63}{100}$ dollars per share be declared and paid to the stockholders of this Academy, or the assignees thereof, and that a written notice of the same be sent by the Finance Committee to such of said stockholders as have not heretofore assigned the surplus of said stock to the Packer Collegiate Institute.

A dividend of $158.63 tells its own story of the financial success the Principal had made of the Academy.

CHAPTER V.

THE PACKER COLLEGIATE INSTITUTE.

A Generous Offer—Erection of the Building—Dedication—Golden Years—Financial Ability—Principles of Government—Anecdotes.

A LIFE of the man who in the mind and estimation of the community is identified with the Packer Institute necessarily includes some mention of the woman to whose enlightened generosity it owes its existence.

This "lady elect" of God, as we believe for this special purpose, a former pupil of the Albany Academy, was early left a widow by William S. Packer, one of the first Board of Trustees of the Brooklyn Female Academy, who showed his complete confidence in his young wife by leaving the control of his large property entirely in her hands. Greatly interested in the education of the young, Mr. Packer had often expressed a desire to do something to promote this object, though he had formed no definite plans in regard to it. The sudden conflagration of the Brooklyn Female Academy seemed to Mrs. Packer to furnish a providential opportunity to carry out these wishes and build at the same time a fitting memorial for her husband. Before the ashes of the old building were cold she had signified her intention of devoting a large sum to its rebuilding and restoration.

A meeting of the Trustees was held on the evening of January 4th, at which was read a note from Mrs. Packer stating that "as she had reason to believe her late husband had entertained the purpose of devoting a sum toward the establishment of an institution for the education of youth, it was her desire as his representative to carry out his wishes." The recent destruction of the building of the Female Academy by fire afforded her an opportunity which she was glad to embrace, and she closed her note by informally offering to devote the munificent sum of sixty-five thousand dollars for the erection of an institution for the instruction of her own sex in the higher branches of education. It is needless to say that this generous offer was gladly accepted.

The Trustees resolved to dissolve the corporation of the Brooklyn Female Academy and apply its stock to the founding of the High School for boys, afterwards known as the Polytechnic Institute. Application was at once made and a grant secured for the incorporation of a girls' academy under the name of the Packer Collegiate Institute, March 19, 1853.

On May 4th the generous originator of the scheme received a copy of the act of incorporation, which she acknowledged by another note to the Trustees, in which she reiterated her offer in due form and expressed "heartfelt thanks for the honor bestowed upon the memory of her husband in giving the Institution his name."

The large sum which the young widow thus put out of her own possession amounted to sixty-five thousand dollars; "a part of which consisted of the grounds and building materials purchased of the Brooklyn Female Academy for the sum of thirty-eight thousand dollars."

Plans of various kinds were at once submitted to both the Trustees and Mrs. Packer, Dr. CRITTENDEN of course taking the greatest interest and offering invaluable suggestions. It was greatly desired by all concerned that the building should be, as Mrs. Packer expressed it, " one with accommodations sufficiently ample to provide for the realization of our most sanguine hopes, and whose style and general appearance would correspond with the character and grade of the school there established. I have thought," she wrote, " that it might tell favorably upon the success of the Institution if the building itself were a kind of token or pledge of the refined and elevated influences to be found within its walls—a pledge I am sure the good management of the Trustees with the blessing of a Higher Power would be able to redeem."

Dr. CRITTENDEN fully agreed with Mrs. Packer's enlightened and far-reaching views; but the Trustees were cautious and hesitated to accept plans " to carry out which might involve the Institution and perhaps materially impair its usefulness;" but again the generous patroness came to the rescue. In another note addressed to the Trustees on May 13th she says:

" I would not have been so decided in favor of Mr. Lefevre's plans had I not first determined to hold myself in readiness to relieve the Institution should it become seriously embarrassed. I hope no such necessity will occur. But if after a sufficient trial the income of the Institution should be found inadequate to provide liberally for its own expenses and make also such provision for a sinking fund as to afford a reasonable prospect of ultimately cancelling the debt, I will engage to add to my donation such sum as may be necessary for this object to the amount of twenty thousand dollars." A document was added in which the writer bound herself, her heirs, executors, administrators, and assigns, to fulfil this voluntary engagement.

Thanks to the wisdom with which the pecuniary affairs of the Packer Institute have always been carried on, and its unexampled prosperity, the additional donation was never claimed; but none the less honor is due to the woman who voluntarily offered *eighty-five thousand dollars* for the elevation and culture of her own sex. Mr. CRITTENDEN thought so, and the tie which bound him to her through life was one of mingled respect, gratitude, and fatherly affection; while on her part love, esteem, and reverence have outlived even his personal presence in our midst.

The way was now open for the erection of the finest building exclusively devoted to female education which the world had at that period seen, for Vassar only existed in the cloudland of its founder's fancies, and Wellesley was an idea unconceived. Mrs. Packer, Mr. CRITTENDEN, and Professor Eaton were not the people to allow an enterprise like this to languish. Money was not spared; the best plans were chosen, the best architects secured, the best heating and ventilating arrangements then known adopted, the handsomest and most durable school-furniture provided, and the laboratory, which Professor Eaton was wont to call his "kitchen," built under his own eye and well stocked with chemicals, minerals, and apparatus of all kinds.

Mr. CRITTENDEN was the life and centre of all the delightful confusion and busy stir. His active brain planned and his strong will secured execution; his habits of economy and his thorough business capacity prevented waste and saved money for the most available purposes. In a

sense the beautiful Phœnix which arose so rapidly
from its own ashes was created by him and created for him : what wonder, then, that the Institution became to him as the years went on his hobby
and idol ; a *bona dea* to which all selfish aims were
subordinated ? What wonder that it was hard for
him to realize the progressiveness of domestic
science, or to allow that any improvements save
those of artistic ornamentation *could* be added to
the "thing of beauty" which was his "joy forever"?

The building, beautiful and complete in its appointments, was finished by the close of the summer vacation, and gave great satisfaction to all
concerned. If some of the "old girls" missed the
light and homely cheerfulness of the old Academy
and thought that in some parts of the building
grandeur was conducive to gloom, we were soon
reconciled to the change, and learned to take
almost as much pride in our beautiful Institution
as our Principal did. On the second Monday in
September, 1854, the Packer Institute was opened
for pupils; but the solemn services of dedication
were not held until the evening of November 9th.

On this occasion the spacious and beautiful Gothic chapel, capable of *seating* one thousand people, was crowded to its utmost capacity, the aisles being filled with seats and standing multitudes thronging the doors and lobbies: a state of things, by the bye, which constantly reproduced itself at every public entertainment of which that chapel was the scene. The galleries were filled with pupils, and multitudes of their friends were unable to obtain admission.

The ceremonies were opened with prayer, after which a richly-embellished and costly copy of the Bible was presented to the institution by Edward A. Lambert, mayor of the city, who accompanied his gift with an appropriate address, to which the President of the Board of Trustees, G. G. Van Wagenen, Esq., made a suitable reply.

The following ode, written by Miss Abby D. Woodbridge, a pupil in the Albany and a teacher in the Brooklyn Female Academy, was sung:

ODE.

Oh ! glad should be our song to-night
　As that which filled the mighty fane
When Hebrews waved the censer bright,
　And swelled the loud exultant strain.
Like them we mourned the wasting fire
Which made our shrine a funeral pyre ;
　Like theirs it rose again !

This " latter house" is very fair,
　Its beauty on our hearts is shed ;
Its name we'll ever keep with care,
　It speaks the living and the dead !
Oh ! 'twas in truth a gracious deed,
The sowing of this precious seed
　For the soul's daily bread.

To Thee, great Source of life and light,
　Kind guardian of each youthful heart
Who here shall seek that second sight
　Which wisdom only can impart,—
For all that makes the soul more pure,
That nerves the spirit to endure,—
　This place is set apart.

'Tis set apart for all that bids
　New thought awake, new purpose live ;
For earth's young flowers, whose dewy lids
　Shut half their sweetness and half give.
Here may the plants of grace abound,
And on this consecrated ground
　May woman learn to live !

The President then formally declared the
building to be specially set apart for the uses

for which it was designed, and addressed the audience.

Rev. Dr. Francis Vinton's magnificent address upon "Female Education" was then delivered. This, having been printed at the time, is within the reach of all our readers. It is a fine presentation of the principles underlying all education, and their modifications when applied to girls. It speaks of the educational improvements which society has recently developed, and using the beautiful new building as an example thereof, closes with a succinct history of its foundation and an eloquent tribute to its founder.

The names of the Board of Trustees as they stood on the night of the opening were:

G. G. VAN WAGENEN,	J. H. PRENTICE,
A. B. BAYLIS,	A. W. BENSON,
C. P. SMITH,	A. A. LOW,
J. SULLIVAN THORNE,	PETER BALEN,
O. H. GORDON,	LOOMIS BALLARD,
PETER C. CORNELL,	B. D. SILLIMAN,
J. W. HARPER,	J. M. VAN COTT,

DAVID COOPE.

At least four of these followed the Principal to

his last resting-place and are still standing man-
fully at their posts.

And now followed thirty golden years; years on
the afternoon side of life, often checkered by
shadows, replete with golden harvests, but full of
seed-sowing still.   Mr. CRITTENDEN never seemed
to grow old; constant association with the young
was to him a perpetual fountain of youth: his
step was as light at seventy as it had been at
seventeen; his eye never lost its clear vision, his
ear its keen sensitiveness to every sound.   Some
of the girls often wished it would.   His executive
ability strengthened with the years, and it was
only towards the very last that he could be in-
duced to lay a few of the cares of government
upon other shoulders and entrust them to other
hands.

Dr. CRITTENDEN was a rare example of a man
who had reached the goal of his ambition.   He
would rather have stood at the head of those hundreds of girls and their teachers than to have
filled any position of public emolument or trust
within the gift of government or society.   It is

therefore matter of congratulation to his old friends that he was able in spite of advanced age and always delicate health to hold his position to the last, and finally to die in harness.

His success in life was not due merely to his scholarship or literary ability; his more effective qualifications were power of discrimination, wisdom in selection, and business capacity. The friend already several times quoted says:

" Mr. CRITTENDEN certainly made the school a financial success. Beginning the Packer Institute with a floating debt of $20,000 and a mortgage of $40,000, he left it free from debt and enriched by greatly increased facilities and a comfortable little sum of $30,000 invested."

The new institution rapidly filled with students, and soon the class-rooms were overflowing. Often over eight hundred names were enrolled in one year, and the teachers multiplied rapidly. In such circumstances the governing power of the Principal stands out conspicuously.

Entirely self-reliant himself, Dr. CRITTENDEN always expected his teachers to be equally so; each sovereign in her own department, as he was

wont to express it. She was expected to govern
by her own inherent force of character, and only
in the last extreme was an appeal to higher authority encouraged; although when such a step
was resorted to it always received a prompt response and the teacher's authority was ably supported. A great weight of responsibility was thus
thrown upon the younger teachers; but the plan
worked remarkably well in the general discipline
of the school.

Also it was his pet boast that the Institution
"governed itself;" "no bells, no rules, as in a
common school." Once an English visitor, admiring the complete appointments of the Packer
and the perfect discipline of its population, asked
him what rules he had.

"None," he answered; "they are not needed.
These young women are ladies; they know what
to do by instinct."

A hobby of Dr. CRITTENDEN'S, which as the
years passed by became almost a mania, was his
unwillingness to dismiss the school for a day or
abridge its sessions for an hour for any reasons
whatever. Until Washington's birthday was de-

clared a legal holiday there was for years an annual contest between the Principal and the school
concerning its observance. "When you can discover the date of *Martha* Washington's birthday,"
he would say, "I promise you a holiday upon that
occasion."

A bright young girl once undertook to write to
Edward Everett for information upon the subject,
but she never succeeded in establishing the anx-
iously-desired date.

On Election-day, observed as a whole or partial
holiday by the public schools, he would say,
"What do you girls want a holiday for? Are you
going to the polls?"

It was the same with all public holidays; even
Sunday-school anniversaries, picnics, and the like;
in fact, no teacher was allowed to excuse a pupil
for any fraction of school time without a written
note from her parent or guardian. Good Friday
and Thanksgiving-day, with the Friday following,
were the only exceptions to this rule; a somewhat
remarkable fact, since Presbyterians in those early
days were not wont to observe church holidays.

Another point on which Dr. CRITTENDEN laid

great stress was the impropriety of allowing a pupil to report herself either as to attendance, deportment, or proficiency in preparation. "It was," he said, "a premium on lying," and on no other occasions was his displeasure towards the teachers so strongly shown or expressed as when they were found guilty of violating this order.

"Success is the test of ability," was one of his favorite mottoes; a hard one to some of the younger teachers struggling with the difficulties of governing undisciplined girls full of high animal spirits, and in many instances not much their juniors. But its application proved its wisdom, and "ability" was cultivated by the necessity for "success."

In fact, under his administration his whole system worked well, and the smoothness with which the wheels revolved which moved this vast aggregation of eight hundred souls was the astonishment of all beholders.

As in the early days, so now, "composition" was Dr. CRITTENDEN'S favorite study. Those who wrote well, especially those gifted with powers of versification, always held a high place in his estimation and a warm one in his heart. He was fond of entertainments, especially if the matter of the dialogues, songs, etc., was of original composition; and the brilliant success of the Packer entertainments is matter of history. He liked to have poems of welcome written when distinguished visitors were expected at the institution, obituaries, Christmas greetings, and the like. He once said of a teacher whose usefulness was apparently on the wane, but who was ready at this sort of thing, "We must keep her, because she brings so much honor to the Institution."

Dr. CRITTENDEN'S jealous care of the property of the Institution will be remembered by many of the pupils, one of whom recalled recently a remark of his concerning some Vandal unknown who had defaced the wall with pencil-marks.

"That young lady is on the road to Blackwell's Island; she *may* never get there, but I wouldn't like to take her chances."

Of the sentimental nonsense which existed, or was supposed to exist, between the elder pupils and the young gentlemen of the Polytechnic, whom they naturally met in their progress to and from school, he was exceedingly intolerant, and on

one occasion politely marshalled two young col-
legians between the serried ranks of six hundred
girls in the chapel, where they were shown to
seats of honor on the platform and compelled to
stand the fire of eyes for a full hour.

Yet no such kindly and genial sympathy was
ever found in the heart of an elder for the real
"affairs of the heart" of his young friends. It was
a pleasure to consult him, and those who did so
were sure alike of shrewd, sensible advice and of
both sympathy and secrecy. He delighted in
weddings, and his gifts upon such occasions were
always beautiful, costly, and well chosen. Towards the inane giggling so dear to the hearts of
school-girls he had a special antipathy, calling it
"the crackling of thorns under a pot," while those
who did not attend to what was going on in class
or chapel were, he said, sending their "fool's eyes
to the ends of the earth."

Every old pupil will remember how frequently
he quoted, "A word to the wise is sufficient; but
you may bray a fool in a mortar, yet will his
foolishness not depart from him."

Dr. CRITTENDEN was always very strict in demanding that those pupils who held scholarships, or were for any reason "free scholars," should make the most of their opportunities and be faithful in obedience to rules. If any of them were caught in the little escapades or instances of resistance to authority common to school life, woe betide them. Some of the more sensitive girls felt this very much; and it sometimes required special exercise of that tact which was his peculiar gift to adjust matters. The following is an illustration:

A young lady holding a scholarship was somewhat remiss, and the teacher of her department chided her, intimating that she expected better things from one in her position. The pupil was indignant, thinking that she was considered a charity scholar, and her father came to complain. Dr. CRITTENDEN received him politely, and, referring to certain rumors then prevalent, said,

"Well, Mr. Smith, will there be war?"

"That depends upon the construction you put on things," he replied.

"That's just it," said Dr. CRITTENDEN. "The teacher said to your daughter, '*considering your position:'* you say, as an object of charity; we say, as a princess—one so distinguished above her classmates as to receive a scholarship; one who we had a right to expect would do better than the others."

CHAPTER VI.

TRAITS OF CHARACTER.

Quick Intuition—Constancy of Friendship—Revivalist—Unlimited Power of Forgiveness—Story of Two Sisters—Judicious
Charity—Repartee—Illustrations.

D R. CRITTENDEN'S many idiosyncrasies of
character came conspicuously to the surface
during these days. He sometimes seemed to be
more largely governed by prejudices or perhaps
one might say by intuitions, than by reason and a
calm weighing of the facts of a case. But his intuitions were usually unerring, and his prejudices
made him a firm and lifelong friend of those to
whom he had taken a fancy, and towards whom he
spared no personal pains when he could be of service to them. Occasionally he seemed to be severe,
especially in what he said at the teachers' meetings. But once when he had been most strictly
holding us to the mark we discovered that he had
been exerting his utmost influence with the Trustees
to secure a rise of ten per cent on all our salaries—

greatly lessened in practical value by the inflation of currency at the close of the war.

There are some men of whom it is said " you always know where to find them." There was sometimes an exciting uncertainty where to find our old friend, which terminated in pleasing disappointment.

On one occasion a noted revivalist with whom she had become acquainted paid a teacher a visit in her school-room. Her own action, seen from a distance, she now feels to have been wholly unjustifiable, completely out of order, and one that might have involved the school in serious consequences. When the excitement consequent upon the personal conversation which she allowed her visitor to have with each of her pupils (very young ones) was reported to her superior and he sent to demand an explanation, she was really afraid to answer the call except by a written account of the whole scene. She waited in some trepidation for a second summons; when entering the room where the Principal sat, he put out his hand kindly and said, pointing to her letter, which he had evidently just read, " I don't understand this thing; were it repeated it might get us into trouble ; but I shan't interfere with it. If children cry because they have told lies and broken rules and not studied their lessons, those are good things to cry about ; but I wouldn't let it happen again."

The Doctor, however, was always very glad to encourage all religious movements which did not interfere with legitimate school discipline and duties. Prayer-meetings were often conducted in the different rooms both before and after school hours; and so long as everything was done " decently and in order" he was very glad that it should be so.

To about this period belongs a personal incident which is a very sweet memory. A member of the school had written a little Christmas poem which was beautifully read by the Reading Teacher, the late lamented Mrs. Perkins, at morning prayers, when the services rather partook of the nature of a celebration.

When, during the morning, the author entered the office, Mr. CRITTENDEN thanked her warmly for it, and, referring especially to its very subjective character, said,

" Do you *always* feel that way ? I would give the world if I could."

One of the old teachers writes:

" Mr. CRITTENDEN seemed to have unlimited power of forgiveness. I think he never harbored a small personal grudge, and so little did he dwell upon personal slights that they soon passed out of his memory; and I have many a time known him positively to forget that certain people had ever manifested an unkind spirit towards him. Nobody could be more generous than he was in repairing an injustice on his own part which had injured another person's feelings. He had also a most generous appreciation of faithful service which he recognized as such. He did not always know how faithful some teachers were, but he was open to conviction where a disinterested party would plead their cause."

An instance of this occurred at one time in connection with a drawing teacher whom he had supposed guilty of want of care of the drawings, casts, etc., provided for the department. With his usual jealous care for the property of the Institute, he spoke quite sharply to her in the presence of her scholars. The writer of the above extract took pains to make him understand how peculiarly careful Miss B—— had been of the articles in question, patching up torn copies and cleaning condemned casts. At once he ran up the five flights of stairs, and before another class of girls said,

"Miss B——, it gives me great pleasure to see your care for the preservation of the models and drawings entrusted to you; you set a good example to all your associates."

During the next summer vacation Dr. CRITTENDEN, hearing that Miss B—— was boarding in the Berkshire Hills, not far from himself and his family, drove over to the village, took the young lady and her sister a long drive, brought them home to dinner, entertained them through the day, and drove them home again by moonlight, "feeling," he said, "that he ought to pay Miss B—— some attention."

The Principal's intense devotion to the Institution has already been noted. He seemed to look upon it almost as if endowed with a soul, to whom others as well as himself were bound to sacrifice themselves.

But wherever school interests did not come into competition, Dr. CRITTENDEN was the most considerate, sympathetic, and helpful of personal friends. He never lost his interest in his old pupils, and looked upon their success in life as personal triumphs. His delight over a successful poem or story or book was intense. On more than one occasion he has fondled a little bantling of a former graduate as though it were a veritable grandchild.

Nor was his sympathy confined to words, as more than one case where sickness and poverty came to some of his protégés can testify. Memory recalls the story of two sisters, members of the graduating class in one of the early years of the Packer, the elder of whom was attacked with hemorrhage of the lungs during one of his recitations. Dr. CRITTENDEN at once took her home in a carriage, and, a little later, sent her South at his own expense. Her disease proved to be old-fashioned consumption, and during her four or five years of gradual fading away he took not only herself but her whole family under his especial protection, sending her to the South every winter establishing her widowed mother in a boarding-house, and giving the second sister the position of book-keeper in the Institute.

And when the fatal disease attacked the younger of the two, he continued to befriend both herself and her mother, till the grave had put an end to all necessity for befriending either. In the pecuniary parts of this enterprise he was assisted largely by Mr. Abraham Baylis and other friends, but the thoughtfulness and care-taking came from his own kind heart.

Mr. CRITTENDEN was a liberal giver of money ; but he gave more than that : he gave personal service, sparing neither pains, time, nor fatigue, and exerting himself to interest others in the objects of his care. This was perhaps one of his chief ways of doing good. He found many ready to give assistance to cases once brought fairly to their notice, and thus was able to accomplish a great deal more than by his own unaided efforts would have been possible. Among those always ready to listen to such appeals and to respond generously to the calls presented was Mr. A. A. Low, now and for many years President of the Board of Trustees.

Many a girl who would otherwise have been obliged to leave the school before her educational course was completed was by Mr. Low's generosity enabled to continue her attendance and secure the diploma which enabled her afterwards to fill an honorable and lucrative position.

The case of the young artist Frederick Bridgman is in point here. Bridgman was a Richmond boy, and Mr. CRITTENDEN was at first interested in him as a fellow-townsman. He, however, early recognized the exceeding promise of the young artist, encouraged his endeavors, and introduced him to the notice of Mr. Low and other gentlemen, who, in conjunction with himself, provided the means to defray his expenses to Europe, and to support him while studying there.

On the return of Bridgman for a short visit to his own country, a reception was given by Dr. CRITTENDEN to the already distinguished artist, and his early friends felt themselves more than repaid for their kindness. The grateful young man never forgot it. Several of his letters have been found among Dr. CRITTENDEN'S few preserved papers; they were written in Paris and

contain many grateful reminiscences. Many allusions to the receipt and sale of Bridgman's pictures
occur in the family correspondence.

The following was written upon the receipt of
the news of Mrs. Crittenden's death, and a much
longer letter of condolence was sent to Mr. Edward Crittenden after that of his father, which,
as it refers to some family matters, can hardly
be inserted here:

75 BOND STREET, PARIS, June 2, 1882.

MY DEAR MR. CRITTENDEN:

If in only a few words, we must tell you how deeply
we feel the loss of one so dear to you all, and how
much we appreciate your having written so soon,
which was a proof that we were among the first in
your mind, though so far away.

F. A. BRIDGMAN.

Dr. CRITTENDEN exerted himself constantly to
procure scholarships for those whose talents and
character promised to make them of use in the
world and an honor to the Institution. In cases
where a change of family circumstances rendered
it impossible for a faithful and ambitious pupil to
complete the prescribed course, he managed in
some way to have her do so, either inducing the

Trustees to cancel the unpaid bills, or paying the arrears himself, or, as frequently happened, calling Mr. Low's attention to the case, etc.; sometimes taking the girls into his own family, where they were considered guests. Indeed, that hospitable household always numbered among its members one or more inmates whose only claims upon it were need of its hospitality.

The following little anecdotes have been sent in as illustrative of the ready wit and quickness at repartee which was at all times one of Mr. CRITTENDEN's distinguishing characteristics:

To a person who asked if there were no elevators in the Institute, he answered, "Yes, madam; each pupil is provided with two."

To the president of a gas company who said there were complaints against the Institute, he replied, "Indeed! Did you ever hear of a complaint against *your* corporation?"

To a physician who wrote to inquire if reduction in tuition would be made to his profession as well as to clergymen, he replied that he regretted to say that reduction was made only to those who preached, not to those who practised.

The following testimonials, which have been contributed by some of his old teachers and friends, tell their own story of the appreciation which those who worked with him had of their Principal :

" For half.a century I have known and respected Mr. CRITTENDEN, having been his pupil, his associated teacher, and for many years his friend and neighbor. In all these relations he was at all times true and steadfast.

" As an educator, his ideas of the dignity of womanhood made him insist upon a course of study which was much in advance of his age. He was blessed with an amount of tact and personal magnetism which enabled him to awaken the youthful mind, teach it to think and arouse it to action. He cultivated not only the intellect, but the conscience and the heart, making his pupils fear to think an unholy or impure thought.

" Many of his pupils, through his generous pecuniary aid, were helped to an advanced education; and they have done good work for the Master whom he loved.

" As a principal, Mr. CRITTENDEN was greatly

respected by his associate teachers. His encouragement and sympathy were never wanting. If they were successful, he usually permitted them to pursue their own methods; but if they needed advice and direction, he gave it with kindness and consideration. He was faithful himself, and exacted the same service for his assistants.

"For almost a quarter of a century we constantly met as friends and neighbors, and never could such be gentler, kinder, more sympathizing than he. I am thankful for his long life of usefulness, and thankful for his death; for he has gone to the reward of those who serve for the love of Christ and in his name."

Another says:

"Mr. CRITTENDEN was one of my kindest, best friends, and I have very much to remember of the courage and happiness he has given to my life. Our intercourse was always of such a personal nature that I do not feel I can recall anything fitted for a public memorial, glad as I am that such is being prepared."

Still another old pupil who has kindly responded to the call for reminiscences says:

"The debt of love and gratitude I owe to Dr. CRITTENDEN is very great; for him I shall ever cherish affectionate remembrance, and hold his memory in highest honor. My youthful admiration of him was sustained by the judgment of maturer years. His most prominent characteristic impressed upon my mind was his strong love of truth and scorn of anything approaching deceit or hypocrisy. The enthusiastic love of truth and goodness because they were beautiful and right in themselves which he felt, he inspired his pupils to feel; and this alone places him in the front rank of the moral educators of the day. While most sincere in condemning an offence, he was even more tender in his forgiveness when penitence was sincere; and if he erred by too hasty a judgment, he was quite as ready to retract and make amends by extraordinary kindness."

Speaking of his father's general popularity and wide acquaintance, Mr. Edward Crittenden says:

"It seemed impossible for my father to go anywhere without finding friends. I have known persons to call within a short time after his arriving at a place hundreds of miles from home, and insist upon his going to their houses. And in business I meet persons who say, 'Your father educated my wife' (or daughter). I am often asked,

"'Are you the son of Dr. CRITTENDEN of the Packer?' 'Oh, yes, we all know him.'

"In Dresden, father, in passing two or three young girls, saw them nudging each other, and overheard them saying, 'Mr. Crittenden.'"

From the same source comes also the following pleasant little incident of travel:

"At church, in London, my father was politely offered a seat by a lady who asked if he were not an American; said she had been delighted with the writings of an American clergyman, Rev. Dr. Sprague. 'He was my former pastor at Albany,' answered my father. 'And then,' continued the lady, 'there is a charming book by another American clergyman, "A Pastor's Sketches,"' 'Yes, madam; Dr. Spencer is my present pastor in Brooklyn.' The lady was surprised, and more so when, in speaking of Dr. Todd, she was told that he and my father were old friends, and had been born in the same town and county."

A pupil of those days says of her old teacher:

" From the time I entered the Institute, in 1874, to the time of his death, his fatherly interest in and tender kindness toward me never ceased. I never failed to find in him a true friend and a wise and judicious adviser. It was his pride and delight to see and watch the progress and assist in the development of a pure and lofty type of womanhood. I cannot tell you in words how much I value his influence as a teacher.

" When visiting the classes in literature he was especially pleased to find students able to give quotations from some of the earlier English authors whose works are now comparatively little studied. On one occasion he called for something from George Herbert. One young lady chanced to repeat,

> " ' A servant with this clause
> Makes drudgery divine ;
> Who sweeps a room as for Thy laws
> Makes that and th' action fine.'

Which more than pleased him."

Mr. CRITTENDEN's faithful friendship for his former pupils is finely illustrated by the following note written to one of them during a protracted illness. A gift of the little volumes "Words of Jesus" and "Faithful Promiser," which accompanied the note, is alluded to therein:

March 8, 1871.

My DEAR FRIEND: Many thanks for your note, and more for the charming poem on prayer. In such a state you cannot be, I trust, very unhappy. I have all day till now anticipated the pleasure of seeing you this P.M., but as it has commenced raining. I send you more comforting "words" than I could speak, and "promises" that He alone who is both able and faithful has given to you and to me. I shall hope to see you the first pleasant afternoon. Till then farewell. May God bless and keep you is the prayer of
Your friend,
A. CRITTEDEN.

Of the same nature is the following, kindly furnished by another old scholar, who says: "This letter beautifully illustrates the ever-ready sympathy which was one of the most lovely elements in the character which made him pre-eminently useful and successful in his profession":

LEE, MASS., August 9, 1875.

My DEAR FRIEND: Your letter of the 2d was received last night.

God is too wise to err, too good needlessly to afflict.

Sickness, desolation of soul, and outward afflictions have all their treasures, though often hidden in dark-ness. But we need not pass through them unblessed.

You have a right to mourn the loss of a kind and loving father, and I am glad to know that you can say, " Thy will be done;" " I would not call him back."

What a consolation it is to you now that you feel no remorse in consequence of a single word or act that gave him pain! May we all thus live, and so fulfil the law of love !

The Lord bless you and keep you in peace !
As ever your friend,
A. CRITTENDEN.

The following résumé of character given by one who knew her subject well during these golden years, but who desires to be nameless, is a faithful picture of the man who stood at the head of the Packer Institute in his ripened age :

" You ask me to jot down some impressions and reminiscences of our dear friend, Dr. CRITTEN-DEN. I first knew him as a pupil, and afterwards more intimately as a friend, during his long resi-dence in Brooklyn.

" His enthusiastic devotion to his profession was always from first to last most noticeable, and I think his great success as an instructor was chief-ly due to this. His influence over his pupils

was both stimulating and inspiring. He had a
happy faculty of making his classes think for
themselves, often throwing aside the text-book
and discussing with them the subject under consideration independently.

"He was quick to discover any special gift or
talent, and many a girl since well known in literature received from him her first encouraging impulse. There was something beautiful in his affectionate interest in those long under his care. Each
graduating class was the best. They were to him
'daughters every one,' as he expressed it the last
time he presented a class to the President for diplomas. This rare insight into character was of great
advantage in the selection of teachers, as witness
the long roll of accomplished women of rare and
varied attainments who were for a longer or
shorter time associated with him in the three institutions over which he presided for more than fifty
years.

"These traits belonged to Dr. CRITTENDEN'S
professional character, but it required the acquaintance and friendship of years to appreciate
his rare geniality of disposition and his real be-

nevolence of heart. Especially was this shown to former teachers or pupils whom sickness or misfortune had overtaken. They instinctively came to him, and he recognized their appeal as a claim upon his time, his purse, and his tenderest sympathy. No amount of personal trouble was too great if he could thereby do them a service. Indeed, I have rarely met his equal in this respect. He never considered the tax upon his time and strength when he could render a service to a friend. Touching instances come to my memory but they are too numerous, and I cannot particularize. Their record is above, where faithfulness to earthly trusts is accounted worthy of great recompense of reward."

CHAPTER VII.

SHADOW AND SUNSHINE.

War Record—Ph.D.—European Trip—His Daughter's Death—
The Silver Wedding.

THE most important public event which occurred during Mr. CRITTENDEN'S long life
was the Civil War of 1861–65. As his attitude
during this trying period has been somewhat criti-
cised, it may be well for a moment to touch upon
issues which are fortunately things of the past.

Always a consistent Democrat, an admirer of
Southern chivalry, generosity, and hospitality,
a believer in States' rights within certain limits,
and a conservative advocate of submission to the
powers that be, he held during the stormy years
that preceded the open declaration of hostilities
a position extremely liable to misconstruction, and
to which many did not hesitate in the heated pas-
sion of after-times to apply the name of *copperhead*.
Looking back, however, through the clarifying
lights of twenty intervening years, it is easy to

see that one simple principle guided all his thoughts and actions throughout these perplexing times—*obedience to law.* So long as the law and government stood, or seemed to stand, upon the side of the unpopular Southern institution which had become a root of bitterness in the community, he persistently discouraged the introduction of the bitter root into his classes or his intercourse with others. But when the advocates of that institution had raised the standard of rebellion and thus put themselves and it without the pale of legal protection, it became the obligation of good citizenship to support with voice, money, and something dearer still the government to which he owed allegiance.

In this there was nothing of the nature of time-service, and his judicious and persistent conduct saved the Institute, at that time somewhat dependent upon Southern patronage, from the evils which violent partisanship might have wrought.

A little incident which occurred just before the firing upon Fort Sumter seems pertinent.

A young friend occupying a position in the school at the time said impulsively,

"Mr. Buchanan is an old grandmother."

"Hush, my child," said the Principal, very gravely; "'the powers that be are ordained of God;' to speak slightingly of them is irreverence to Him. I hope never again to hear such words from your lips."

"My father," says the son who was one with him in opinion, "though not a partisan, was a Democrat in politics. When no important issue seemed to be involved in an election he voted for the candidate whom he considered the best man, without regard to party. I have known him to refuse to vote for a candidate of either party because he knew and could ascertain nothing about him. On the question of slavery, he esteemed the institution an evil, but one concerning which, under the Constitution, neither the government nor any free State had anything to do. He was unequivocally a Union man. He thought the States had rights that the general government had no business to meddle with, and in the excitement which followed upon the firing upon Sumter the expression of such opinion was by some deemed disloyalty."

From that crisis, however, no one could doubt the loyalty of the Principal and all engaged in the Institution. The attitude taken and maintained throughout the war was unmistakable. Political partisanship was not encouraged in a community most of whose members neither were nor expected to be enfranchised citizens; but woman's war-work was carried on: lint was scraped, bandages rolled, "comfort-bags" prepared, and stockings knit, even within those sacred precincts devoted to more masculine pursuits; the rules which forbade the introduction of such femininities into chapel, class-rooms, and recitations being, with the full approbation of the Principal, relaxed in favor of the defenders of our Union. Red, white, and blue were as conspicuously displayed in the Packer Institute as elsewhere in the city; its windows were as often illuminated; entertainments were given for the benefit of the sufferers on both sides, and at the great fair held in aid of the Sanitary Commission in the Academy of Music the "Packer Table" was a prominent feature and added several thousand dollars to the general fund; teachers and older scholars being spared from their daily duties to take charge of the sales.

When the great excitement of the end came, no one took part in the brief outburst of joy over Lee's surrender and the anguish which almost instantly shrouded the nation at the fate of the first martyr-President with more intense earnestness than the Principal of the Packer Institute, who at once dismissed the school, not to reassemble until after the public funeral; a sacrifice of a pet theory which we who were intimately acquainted with him knew how to appreciate.

Nor did Mr. CRITTENDEN spare his own to the country's needs when the time came for the sacrifice. His only son, then a member of the 23d Regiment, N. Y. S. M., was ordered to Harrisburg, opposite which he was encamped in June, 1863. Several letters to him full of fatherly solicitude mingled with willing devotion to the public good are to be found among Mr. CRITTENDEN's papers.

Just before the close of the war, January 12, 1865, the respected Principal received that which he considered as the greatest of honors—the degree of Doctor of Philosophy, conferred by the regents of the University of the State of New York. This he considered a much more honorable degree than one bestowed by a mere college, since the regents govern the colleges.

His reverence for "the regents" was extreme. Both scholars and teachers learned from him to look upon them in the light of superior beings, and a "regents' examination" was invested with a formality usually accorded to royalty. The new title was easily adopted by new-comers, and by the time of Dr. CRITTENDEN's death had become universal in the school of that day; but to some of us early pupils the change was hard to make, and our old friend is *Mr.* CRITTENDEN to us to this day.

But the golden days were before long succeeded by darker ones. The health of the lovely and accomplished daughter, always the joy and delight of her father's heart, once more began to fail. She was now a young wife and mother, and the hearts of a whole family circle were stirred with anxiety for the precious life. Physicians advised an entire change of air

and scene, and the Principal himself, needing a
period of rest and relaxation after so many years
of close devotion to his work, applied for leave
of absence, which the Trustees gladly granted,
and the whole family went abroad.

The following answer to the letter of application is presented to the reader in token of the
high appreciation in which the Principal was held
by those to whom he was directly responsible:

May 28, 1867.

*To Alonzo Crittenden, Esq., Principal of the Faculty of
Instruction of the Packer Collegiate Institute.*

DEAR SIR: The Board of Trustees at their meeting
this evening appointed us to communicate to you an
expression of their respect for you personally, and of
their sense of the important services you have rendered to the cause of female education, here and elsewhere, as the head of two important academic institutions. We hope that your absence will insure you
that repose which long and faithful labors so well
deserve, and that you will return to us renewed in
health and strength, and confirmed in your devotion
to the interests to which you have dedicated so large
a portion of your life.

Truly yours,   JOHN H. PRENTICE,
President pro tem.

J. SULLIVAN THORNE,
JOHN HASLETT,   } *Committee.*
ABRAM B. BAYLIS,
JOSHUA M. VAN COTT.

Before leaving home, Dr. CRITTENDEN seemed to feel some apprehension that he never should return; his manners became more than usually affectionate and tender, and his chapel-prayers more fervent. He sent for each teacher in turn, gave her earnest advice and counsel, and parted from her as though she had been his daughter in deed. He had little anxiety about leaving the school under the able superintendence of Professor Eaton; indeed, so thoroughly were the wheels of government organized that the school might have run itself, as it did for several months the winter of his death, when the Professor too, stricken down with an apparently mortal illness, lay upon a sick-bed at Asheville, N. C.

During the whole period of absence, protracted because of the continuous and increasing illness of the object of his solicitude, the absent Principal wrote weekly letters which were read aloud to the whole school, and in this way we followed him all along a tour which included England, Ireland and Scotland, Holland, Germany, Switzerland, France, and Italy. Pauses longer or shorter were made at all the principal points of interest,

and early in November the party reached Mentone on the Mediterranean, where the invalid was
housed for the winter.

Here Mrs. Crittenden, Mr. and Mrs. Dana,
and the children remained, while Dr. CRITTEN-
DEN, his son, and Miss Clara Talcott—a relative
who afterwards died very suddenly while filling
the position of a teacher in the Institute—made a
tour in Italy, one of the party even crossing over
into Africa.

It was a sad winter that followed for the party
at Mentone, the sadness culminating when on
March 3d Mrs. Dana passed away. Of the grief
of that parting in a strange land no written traces
seem to have been preserved. The father's heart
was almost broken ; the mother received her death-
blow, from which she never entirely rallied, taking henceforth the place of the family invalid, to
be tenderly cared for and guarded by the husband
whose heart was so entirely hers.

The homeward journey commenced March 13th,
and was taken in a somewhat leisurely fashion.
From Paris, which was reached August 6th, Mr.
Edward Crittenden returned to Mentone for the

remains of his sister, which he took to Havre, sailing for New York August 30th, while the rest of the party, crossing to England again, travelled through Wales, and sailed from Liverpool, reaching home in time for the opening of the fall term at the Institute.

Of the exceedingly interesting correspondence of those eighteen months scarcely anything can be found. A long letter sent by Professor Eaton to the absent Principal still exists. It is written on thirty-eight thin sheets by thirty-eight different teachers. The sheets are pasted together and rolled like those of an ancient manuscript. It would be interesting, did space allow, to publish the whole; it would be invidious to make selections. A few allusions to Dr. CRITTENDEN's travels appear in family letters, especially those written to his son concerning the interment of his daughter, and the kindness received from friends in England when visiting it for the second time under such sad auspices.

A pleasant feature of this European tour was the many friends new and old whom the party was constantly making and meeting. The follow ing remembrance of one of these meetings has just been received. Its writer was a pupil in the Albany and a teacher in the Brooklyn Female Academy.

"In the autumn of 1868 Dr. CRITTENDEN was one of a party of seven with whom I travelled over the Corniche road. We were five days in an Italian carriage, and I have no recollection of him more vivid than when on that fifth day we ascended a spur of the Maritime Alps on our way to Spezzia.

"It was Sunday. No one of the party but felt it wrong to travel on that day, but we had been strongly tempted. Our inn was uncomfortable from draughts and stony floors, the table wretched, and our host brigandish. As we ascended, our views were magnificent, the air clear and frosty, and the roadside chapels receiving and sending forth devout and picturesque worshippers.

"In these calm heights our friend discoursed on subjects of interest in life and literature. He repeated a sacred poem, the production of a mutual friend, and our day was one of great enjoyment.

"Mrs. Dana was at this time at Mentone, and

Mrs. Crittenden was anxiously watching over her while her husband took this journey for rest and refreshment.

" From my early childhood I had known these dear friends, and my regard increased with years."

The home-coming of the stricken family was a sad one, but the heart of the returning School Father was gladdened by the warm welcome of his flock. A reception was held in the chapel of the Institute; several school poets expressing their affection in verse.

The "Silver Wedding" of the Institution (Female Academy and Packer Collegiate Institute combined) was celebrated in the summer of 1871. The exercises lasted nearly a week. There was a junior exhibition; a "Class Day" entertainment; a "Founder's Day;" the Commencement proper (which was held in Dr. Storrs's church); an evening entertainment given by Mrs. Packer; an afternoon reception at Mr. Low's for the teachers and senior class; and a distinct anniversary meeting in the Academy of Music, at which George William Curtis delivered the address.

On the closing evening the whole Institute

building, brilliantly lighted and beautifully decorated with pictures, statues, and flowers, was
thrown open to many hundreds of invited guests,
who were received by Mrs. Crittenden with stately courtesy and Mrs. Packer with unaffected grace.
About three hundred of the Alumnæ were present, and many broken ties were reunited as groups
of old friends met together to recall the well-
remembered scenes and incidents of days gone
by. The assemblage was brilliant in the extreme.

In the course of the evening a marble statue of
Rev. Dr. Bethune, which still stands in the main
entrance-hall, was unveiled, Rev. Dr. Vinton deliv-
ering a brief address. During this address, Dr.
CRITTENDEN, who had throughout the evening
seemed radiant with happiness, beckoned to several of us to follow him quietly into the apartments he then occupied, where, dropping on a
sofa, he was seized with the first of those sinking
turns the recurrence of which later ended in his
death. One of his peculiar traits impressed itself
on this occasion. Partially recovering, he said
to one, who was bending over him, "Don't let
Mrs. Crittenden know; she is not strong enough

to stand shocks." Later in the evening, having to all appearance completely recovered, he stood upon the platform in the dear old chapel to receive with graceful gladness the beautiful testimonial gift in which many hearts had gladly united. Professor Eaton opened the mysterious box which had already excited the curiosity of many and disclosed a magnificent service of plate, the gift of the Alumnæ and some of their friends. It was afterwards discovered that some one had privately conveyed to the recipient an intimation of the honor he was to receive, and his feelings completely overcoming him had caused the previous attack of prostration.

The presentation was accompanied by a brief but eloquent speech from the Professor, who also read an impromptu poem entitled "Our Alma Mater," written by one of the Alumnæ. This was certainly the moment of the successful Principal's highest triumph. He stood surrounded by the sheaves of his twenty-five years' seed-sowing and harvesting; he had reached the goal of his ambition; he was crowned with the bays woven by respect, appreciation, and gratitude; his cup

was full, but he emptied it as a libation at the feet
of his *Bona Dea*, the Institution, and felt the triumph to be hers rather than his own.

OUR ALMA MATER.

Lo! once more gathered in our hall,
   A broken yet united band,
We come responsive to that call
   Which, echoing widely o'er our land,
Has bade us celebrate to-night
Our Alma Mater's birthday bright.

It rolled along the prairied West;
   Its Southern echo from the sea
Was wafted upward to the crest
   Of Eastern hill and midland lea:
And wearing still our mother's chain,
We heard her mandate not in vain.

Hand has met hand in loving grasp,
   Bright smile has answered to bright smile,
Time has prevailed not to unclasp
   The golden bands forged here erewhile,
And memory's magic touch can bring
Even to August breaths of spring.

We have brought with us chastened hearts,
   Fresh-springing blades and ripening ears,
Deep channels furrowed by the parts
   Each one has played these busy years;
Our gathered sheaves we fain would lay
Upon our mother's shrine to-day.

Yet while the star of home may be
    Its mother-love, a beacon-light
Guiding across life's stormy sea
    Its loved ones to their harbor bright,
Before we pass the threshold o'er
A *father's* blessing guards the door.

Our father! to thy patient care
    Our Alma Mater owes its fame;
And thou art honored everywhere
    That floats the echo of her name.
We greet to-night with loyal pride
Our father and his silver bride.

Not daughterless thou art e'en here,
    Although above these summer skies
Two radiant forms be waiting thee
    Robed in the hues of paradise:
For thee a daughter's bosom glows
In every State our Union knows.

We are not all sweet maidens fair,
    Our youth is gliding swift away,
As raven tress and golden hair
    O'er many a brow is streaked with gray;
To-night such tokens speak in vain,
To thee we are but girls again.

Girls in the grateful love which lays
    Before thy feet our little all;
Girls in the shy half-uttered praise
    Which on thy heart like dew may fall;
As incense from the fresh June flowers
Wafts back the fragrance of her showers.

Thy words have been in many a fight
　The conquering legend on our shield ;
And oft in sorrow's stormy night,
　Held where all other anchors yield,
Thy hands have clasped our casque and mail
And trimmed our vessels for the gale.

So as to-night we meet to keep
　With joyful hearts our mother's day,
To *him* who up the rugged steeps
　Of learning led our onward way,
To him we fain would offering bring
As at his feet our thanks we sing.

Accept our gift !　Not metal base ;
　Sacred as mediæval shrine,
More precious than Etruscan vase,
　Love sought the treasure in the mine.
To eyes that loving see aright
This silver hath celestial light.

We cannot thank thee : only pray
　For sunset brighter far than dawn ;
That He who led thee all life's way
　May ope at last the gates of morn,
Then bid thine opened vision see
All that thy daughters owe to thee.

　　　　　　　　　　　　　M. E. W.

CHAPTER VIII.

THE LAST DECADE.

Home Life—Somerville—Rothstein Lodge—A New Daughter—
Correspondence—The Milton Shield—Signing his Will.

SOME men there are who seem to have drunk
deeply of the fountain of perpetual youth:
years do not sour them; time does not silver them;
their eyes are not dim; their natural force is
scarcely abated. No one who knew ALONZO CRIT-
TENDEN during the ten or twelve years which inter-
vened between the "silver wedding" and his death
ever thought of him as an *old* man.

He had repeated illnesses, generally attacks of
difficult breathing, possibly, as physicians now
think, of the same heart-trouble which finally
caused his death; but on the whole he filled
his old place in the school, and though he no
longer taught classes, the Institute felt his individuality as strongly as ever. But there was
a change in him which every one saw and felt:

there was a certain tremulousness of hand which led him generally to dictate his letters, although when he did write them himself the penmanship was as clear and characteristic as ever, and the signature had lost nothing of its firmness. He began to lean insensibly upon the judgment of others, finding substantial aid and support in Professor Eaton and Miss Susan K. Cook, head of the collegiate department.

But more and more his heart seemed to turn to his home life, with its sweet duties and healthful cares; above all, its broad hospitalities. Providence had favored him, as it always does those of good business ability,—with more than a competence, and the comforts he was able to secure were for everybody's benefit as much as his own.

As early as 1850 he had become possessed of about one hundred and eighty acres of land in Westchester County, between Bronxville and Mount Vernon, on which stood a small old farmhouse, which he remodelled in English style and named Somerville Cottage. This farm was one of three given by government to the captors of Major André, and thus possessed historic interest in addition to the beauty of its situation and the charm conferred by its unbounded hospitality.

Here he removed his family in early spring every year, going out himself as soon as school closed on Friday afternoons and coming in early on Monday morning—always, however, reaching the Institute in time for prayers. The commodious "cottage" was generally filled to overflowing, and nowhere were guests so royally entertained. Legends of these festivities are still extant, in especial of one grand sleigh-ride in which Rev. Dr. S. I. Prime, Dr. Haslett, and several other distinguished Brooklynites were with 'their families transported to the comfortable mansion. Here they found warm fires and a warmer welcome prepared for their reception by the cousin who presided over the household in the absence of its mistress, spent a gay evening and a comfortable night, and were in the morning carried merrily back to town.

Later the old farm was sold, and a beautiful place was purchased from the Rev. Dr. Eels at Englewood, New Jersey, and thither the family was transported, hospitality and all. This house was one of those old New Jersey stone mansions modernized, and received from its new owner the name of Rothstein (red stone) Lodge. It was bought chiefly with a view to the recuperation of Mrs. Dana's already failing health; and although she did not live long to enjoy it, its owner took great delight in his fields and his gardens, his cattle and his fruit. The writer remembers with great pleasure three brilliant autumn days spent by her and her sister at this delightful mansion. Its kind hosts devoted themselves to the entertainment of their guests, showing them of the beautiful palisade country

> "As much as two strong *horses*
> Could *do* from morn till night."

In winter these same horses were used in the city for everybody's convenience. Invalid friends were taken to drive; the carriage was placed at the service of those in affliction; it was seen at funerals, especially of the poor, who otherwise had had few followers.

The family circle consisted for a time of Dr. and Mrs. CRITTENDEN, their son, their son-in-law and his two motherless little girls, to whom their grandmother was a second mother. To this happy home party was added in 1872 a young lady from Wayne, N. Y., who in becoming Mr. Edward Crittenden's wife became also the sunshine of the home, fitting into the lost daughter's place, and becoming in time emphatically the "old man's darling." Most of the letters from his pen which have been preserved are to this beloved daughter and her children, as one by one they came to call out still more his wealth of affection; and among the last of his intelligible sentences was the following, addressed to her,

"I can die in perfect peace, trusting to your good judgment and discretion."

The following welcome awaited his son and daughter on their return from their wedding trip :

September 17, 1872.

MY DEAR CHILDREN :

I have a presentiment that you will return to-day ; and I regret more than you know that I shall not be here to receive and bid you welcome. And worse than all, your good mother will not have the pleasure, the very great pleasure, both you and she anticipated of extending to you both the right hand of truth, and of pressing you to a heart glowing with love.

I must go back to my work for just a little time longer, and I am sorry that I feel so illy able to perform it. But you must not be anxious on my account. God bless you, my dear children. May the burdens of life be lighter to you both than they possibly could have been had you not resolved to share them together! Your devoted FATHER.

On receiving the announcement of the birth of his first grandson he wrote to the happy father:

October 31, 1873.

I have just received your telegram. Your mother is overcome with joy. She said, "Down upon your knees and thank God." A. C.

On October 4, 1877, he thus announces to his daughter the deaths of two who had been long and intimately associated with the Packer:

October 4, 1878.

We carried our dear friend Dr. Haslett to his final resting-place last Sunday. To-day we pay our token of respect and sympathy to a former and beloved co-worker, Miss Louise Van Ingen. So we are passing over one by one, and soon we shall all be there; may it be where there is no more sorrow, no more sin!

From one of the longest and most interesting of his letters still remaining, the following, also addressed to his daughter, will be found of great interest :

Sunday, September 22, 1878.

The service is over and the dinner, and I am at my table to close this note commenced this morning. The text was, "And every one shall give an account of himself to God," a solemn and admonitory sermon from our good little minister, Mr. Booth. May we all so live that we can give the account with joy, receiving the welcome, "Well done, good and faithful servant" !

It is a serious matter when we live simply in reference to our own individual welfare, but frightful when we consider the influence our conduct may have upon the destiny of our children and others whom we influence. It is my constant prayer, Leave us not alone to ourselves.

. . . .

I am determined, if perseverance can accomplish it, to get my affairs so arranged that they will give me less trouble and be less likely to trouble others. Delay, especially when interest is concerned that knows *no delay*, has ruined thousands.

I read in the chapel the other morning the 25th chapter of Matthew, and then referred to the yellow-fever in the South ; the destitution and the need of clothing. In forty-eight hours some 125 bundles of clothing were sent to the Institute contributed by gay ladies. Was it not noble ? yes, glorious ? Poor desolate South ! How chastened, and how liberal the contributions from the North ! New York alone has raised three quarters of a million of dollars. I do not believe that nobler or more generous men live on this round earth than are to be found in this city. A. C.

Another letter will help to show the pleasant relations existing between the father and daughter:

To his Daughter-in-law.

Your mother loves you all quite as much as she should, but she says more of "my boy" than of the other, who I wish you to understand is "*my* boy." Lo! what will you and their father do?

Well, we will be as considerate and kind as Pharaoh's daughter, and let you nurse the boys, and we trust they will have such training as will qualify them to find their way through the wilderness of sin.

.   .   .   .

The Good Father knows best, but I had not thought, my dear Margaret, that you needed this severe discipline. Yet you may (see Heb. xii. 6). After all the experiments that have been made since the world was created to secure comfort under trial and consolation under all circumstances, there is but one unfailing source (1st Tim. i. 15). . . .

Do you remember Dr. Storrs's sermon on the dignity of labor? (Mal. xx. 28.) You are in a condition to make a trial, and I hope you will find yourself benefited by your work. If you can feel the rock of ages your support, you will not fail.

You don't know how dearly your mother (step) loves you. Are you not fortunate in having two such mothers? Better than to have *forefathers.*

The following extracts from letters written to Dr. Crittenden's grandchildren during the closing years of his life, present so beautiful a picture of the loving heart chastened and ripened by age and discipline, yet living a renewed youth in the young life of a third generation, that it has seemed no violation of the sanctities of home to lay them before an appreciative public of old scholars and warm friends, for whom chiefly this volume has been written. The quaintly characteristic addresses are the grandfather's own.

To Samuel Hallett Crittenden.

December 25, 1878.

THE DEAR PRECIOUS CHILD SAMUEL: May you early hear the voice of the Lord calling you into His service, and may you say "Here am I"!   GRANDPA.

To Masters Edward, Alonzo, and Hallett Crittenden.

Isle of Shoals, Portsmouth, N. H.,
July 3, 1879.

My Dear Little Men:

.   .   .   .

When we get home I shall tell you all about these strange isles, and about a most strange man with a strange name—John Smith—who discovered them almost three hundred years ago. He made a map of the region, went back to England, was a great sailor, mariner, and famous in many ways. . . .

When you learn the strange history of Smith, and of

others like him, you will be prepared to travel with interest and profit. . . .

People may be happy in almost any condition if they are good and amiable, for then they will have friends who will make them happy almost in spite of themselves. But if you expect to have friends to make you happy, you must take care to make others happy, and this you cannot do without often giving up what seems to be the most desirable for the pleasure or good of others. I have never been so proud of Edward as when he has given up to Alonzo simply because he was the youngest. But Alonzo will soon learn that he cannot enjoy anything that will give others pain or even inconvenience to yield. . . .

May the loving Father bless you and make you His own dear children!   GRANDPA.

To Master Edward Crittenden.

August 15, 1880.

.   .   .   .

And now, my little man, how do you feel in view of the responsibilities you have assumed as the protector of your mother and exemplar to Hallett and your little sister?

Your dear mother has a right to look to you now for assistance, aid, and comfort, as hereafter she will for protection.

At your age it will often be hard for you to discharge all the duties you owe to your mother, brothers and little sister, to yourself, and to your Heavenly Father, the giver of all you have or all you may expect to have. I have often told you that you must be a model, for your brothers and little sister will be like you in character. It will be hard at times; . . . but just make the experiment, and then you will know whether you have greater pleasure in pleasing others or yourself. The pleasantest rides I have ever had have been when I have given my horse to another and walked myself.

. . . .

Some men and women often when they have done wrong or acted wickedly resort to falsehood to cover their folly and shame, but they never succeed. The trouble is *they* know it, and God knows it; they lose all respect for themselves, and cannot expect favor from God or man. Truthfulness is the foundation of a noble and manly character, and the want of it destructive of all that is desirable in this life or life everlasting. And then let me commend to you another element of a noble and manly character—honor and respect to parents. Ask your mamma to repeat to you the fifth commandment, and read what the wise man says in Prov. xxx. 17. You cannot obey the fifth commandment without cheerful and prompt obedience. A. C.

To the Precious Little Pearl [Margaret].

December 25, 1880.

Blessings on you, our little Pearl! God grant in mercy that you may live to be all that your father, mother, and other friends, and that we anticipate!

GRANDPA AND GRANDMA CRITTENDEN.

To Edward H. Crittenden.

December 25, 1880.

DEAR EDWARD: Ever bear in mind that "life will be what you make it." Persistent people begin their success where others end in failure. GRANDPA.

December 25, 1880.

To Alonzo the Brave—Ever Ready.

My Dear Namesake: Be good and you will be happy. Ever remember that the reward of virtue is virtue. And if you would have friends be one. You have the blessing of grandpa and grandma. May God add His, which is far better!

To Master Hallett.

December 25, 1881.

Dear Hallett: If you wish to have the means of making others happy, take care of the pennies.

This is one way; a better one is to be cheerful and happy yourself.

May the good Father always have you in His keeping!   Grandpa.

During these years Mrs. Crittenden's health was continually failing. She never entirely recovered from the strain of that sad winter at Mentone, and she became a constant and confirmed invalid. Much of her husband's time and thoughts were taken up with care for her comfort and temporary relief. Several successive winters southern trips were undertaken with this end; they seemed to greatly benefit Dr. Crittenden himself, who always came back invigorated and rejuvenated. He came back also completely *au fait* at everything which had occurred in the school during his absence, and ready to resume the reins as though they had never been dropped.

It was during the first of these Southern trips that he wrote to his son :

April 16, 1870.
Your letter bearing the sad intelligence of dear Clara's death was received last evening.

Your indorsement on the envelope was considerate, as it prepared us for the tidings.

.   .   .   .

A death like this to one so ripe for heaven is beautiful. What a transition from earth to heaven, from pain to praise !

Considering all the circumstances, who of all who loved and admired her character can doubt that for her " to die is gain" ? No one out of our own immediate family was nearer or dearer to us than Clara ; and we cannot desire to have it otherwise. It is " far better" that she should " depart" and be with her Saviour.

The reader will remember that Miss Clara Talcott was one of the European party. Like her cousin she died in harness, having stood faithfully at her post in the Institute until five o'clock in the afternoon, and receiving her summons to " come up higher" at midnight of the same day, March 14, 1870.

It was on one of these southern trips also that
Dr. CRITTENDEN renewed his intimacy with his
Greenville friend, an extract from whose tribute
of affectionate appreciation was given in the earlier
pages of this memorial. He henceforth kept up
with her a constant and interesting correspondence, concerning which she writes:

"The happy faculty he had of recollecting that
which was pleasant is illustrated in the following
extract from one of his letters: 'Mrs. S. made a
short call yesterday, and gave occasion to revive
old scenes of lang syne—the pleasant time we
spent at G., your visit to R. L., and recollections
of long ago. How grateful we should be that we
are so constituted that we can live over and over
again the pleasantest parts of our lives! Almost
every week I make the whole tour of Europe just
in an hour with a friend, and thus we have made
you all at G. and P. a visit.'

"Another extract shows how he thought we
should receive our blessings: 'I am quite delighted to know that you are so comfortably situated;
free from care; have so many dear ones around
you. All this, and heaven besides! What can

you desire more? It must be your own fault if
you are not happy.'

"Another suggestion in one of his letters is,
'Cheerfulness is the best medicine, and I hope you
will take it, well shaken up by hearty laughs, morning, noon, and night.'

"And still another gives expression to his untiring, active, and buoyant spirit: 'It is a good
thing that we are all too busy to grow old.'

"I regret that many of his letters are packed
away beyond reach at this time, or other characteristics could be brought out from many terse
ejaculatory sentences, in which good counsel, reverent submission to the Divine Will, cheerful encouragement, sprightly allusions and playful remarks all had their part. His was a life so full of
youth that to be with him was to throw off care.
Such a life can never entirely pass out of the lives
of those who follow him."

In August, 1879, occurred the fiftieth anniversary of the marriage of Dr. and Mrs. CRITTENDEN.
A golden-wedding celebration was proposed, and
for some time under consideration in the family.
The plan was, however, abandoned, partly in con-

sideration of Mrs. Crittenden's delicate health, partly because the season was one when most of the family connections were out of town.

Many friends, however, sent congratulatory letters and notes, and Professor Horsford, whose friendship, commenced so long ago in Albany, had never been cooled by years, accompanied his letter by a gift of the Milton Shield, a beautiful disk of metal on whose surface some of the chief scenes from " Paradise Lost" are embossed.

Dr. CRITTENDEN was greatly delighted with and highly prized this beautiful gift. Meeting a friend soon afterward, he insisted on taking her home with him to inspect it and listen to its history. At his death he bequeathed it to the Institute.

Professor Horsford's esteem and admiration of his early friends continued unabated to the end. On hearing that Mrs. Crittenden would in all probability die, he wrote, under date of

May 2, 1882.

MY POOR DEAR FRIEND :

I have your sad letter. It is inexpressibly sad, but, my dear friend, what infinite mercies have been yours ! How long the blessed companionship, the common sweet memories, the privileges of mutual trust and service have been vouchsafed to you ! Think of this, and know in spite of the darkness there is infinite wisdom beyond. . . .

I have been so much in the presence of the pro-cession going over to the other side for the last few months, it does not seem as far to the end as it once did. . . . Affectionately yours,

E. N. HORSFORD.

To the story of the year 1880 belongs this touch-ing incident, communicated by Mrs. Roger A Pryor to Mr. Edward Crittenden, and now pub-lished by his kind permission :

SIGNING HIS WILL.*

" BROOKLYN, May 17, 1881.

" The circumstances attending the writing and' signing of Dr. CRITTENDEN'S will seem to me so solemn and interesting that I have resolved to write them while they are fresh in my memory.

" One evening in December, 1880 (I forget the precise date), Mr. Pryor came to me while I was conversing with some guests in my parlor. He said, 'You must excuse yourself for a few min-utes ; I need you in the library.'

---

* The will signed upon this occasion was not a final one.

" Upon reaching the library I found Dr. CRIT-
TENDEN, who immediately said to me,

" ' I wish you to witness my will. You see, my
young friends, I give you my confidence.' Then
turning to me, he said pleasantly, ' You know you
have the pen of a ready writer.'

" My husband put the usual questions to him,
and I wrote what was dictated to me and signed
the will.

. " He came again to our house on the evening of
Mr. John Bullard's funeral, and was much dis-
turbed at finding Mr. Pryor absent. He said to
me very earnestly, ' I must add a codicil to my
will, and you must witness it. I cannot rest until
I get my house in order.'

" We did not hear from him again until the
first of May. He called frequently, but Mr. Pryor
was out of the 'city, and I promised to let him
know the moment my husband returned. He then
said, ' I must trouble you again; I have written my
will all over.'

" He was impatient about my husband's absence
and sent several times to know if he had returned.
Finally Mr. Pryor arrived, and I immediately noti-

fied him of the fact. He came at once, bringing the new will. He left it with us for an hour. and returning, said, ' I have altered my will. I wish to direct my executors so that those who come after me will have no trouble and no perplexity.'

"After the will was signed he became very cheerful. He talked happily about his failing health, telling of his difficulty in breathing. Mr. Pryor's attention was attracted by his unusual spirits, and he said, ' You seem, sir, to look upon death with great serenity.'

" ' I do, I do,' replied Dr. CRITTENDEN. ' I have no fears, no sad thoughts; my house is in order. He presently added, ' In this matter I have counselled with you alone; I owe you more than thanks.'

" My husband replied, ' We are honored; you owe us nothing, not even thanks ; we are only too glad to serve you.'

"I was sitting across the room a little to his right, the library-table being between us, and he leaned over and looked at me, saying, ' Why, your face wears a *minor* expression ! It is usually *major ;* why is this ?'

"I replied, 'The occasion is sad and mournful to me, dear Mr. CRITTENDEN.'

"He laughed lightly and said, 'Oh, no! oh, no!'

"Writing this, I feel that my words have not conveyed the impression of peace, serenity, and cheerfulness which his manner gave us. When he left, Mr. Pryor said, 'A noble, honorable man; a man who need not fear death.'

"SARA AGNACE PRYOR."

Accompanying the above statement Mrs. Pryor sent the following note, received by her the day after Dr. CRITTENDEN's birthday and alluding no doubt to the signing of his will:

4. 8. 80.

DEAR MRS. PRYOR:

I was greatly gratified with your note of congratulations yesterday. It was to me a sadly pleasant day.

It should not have had an element of sadness. The setting sun of so long a day should pillow its head upon the gold and azure, the harbingers of a day that knows no night.   A. CRITTENDEN.

CHAPTER IX.

A SAD SPRING-TIME.

The Last Birthday—Estimate of an Old Teacher—A Base Attack —Offers his Resignation—Trustees Refuse to Accept—Letter from Professor Eaton—Death of Mrs. Crittenden—The Alumnæ Association.

THE year 1882 was the last of Dr. CRITTEN-DEN'S life, and on the whole the saddest. There are golden summer days whose early showers have long since cleared away, whose noontide has been sunny, and whose afternoon mellow, into which, just before sunset, there often comes a thunder-storm, sent as it were to afford a background on which might be painted the glowing rainbow of promise for the coming morrow. Such a dark background did Dr. CRITTEN-DEN'S last year furnish for the glory beyond.

Mrs. Crittenden's health had been for some years steadily failing ; his own was far from good. Hand in hand the faithful couple were descending the last slope which led to the shadowy river, and the chief care of each was to make the descent of the other as easy as possible, while daily sowing seeds of sweet, bright memories to grow up and bear precious fruit in the hearts of the dear ones so soon to be left behind. Mrs. Crittenden's family letters of that period, of which many have been preserved, are full of a lovely Christian spirit which told of well-improved discipline and increasing ripeness for heaven. In the midst of her weakness she still wrote frequently, even attempting, from time to time, some playful little verses to accompany a gift or tribute of affection. The last birthday letter to her husband which has been preserved is as follows:

MY DEAR OLD HUSBAND: April 7.

I cannot let this day pass without thanking you for all your devotion and kindness to me, unvaried through my married life, and still increasing as my health and strength seem to depart from me.

I have no offering but that of a grateful, loving heart ; but may God bless you for "all your labors of love," and illumine your later years with His approving smiles and blessings !

YOUR AIN AULD WIFE.

That last birthday was a green one in the Doctor's life. Teachers, pupils, and friends vied with each other in the presentation of good wishes and notes, fruits and flowers. Flora seemed to have decorated the Institute, and Pomona to have piled the office table with her choicest gifts. The old man was young again in his joy.

Hearing of the ovation, a friend, once connected with the Institute, sent him next day a copy of her last book, with a playful little note which said :

" Fruits and flowers have I none ; but such as I have send I unto thee. Please accept the grandchild of the Institute."

He was greatly delighted with this little gift ; carried it from room to room, reading the note to the teachers, and telling the pupils that that was the kind of thing to be expected of them. He also sat down and wrote the author an autograph note of thanks—the last she ever received from him—which closed with the words :

" I hope you will always find the secret of victory [the title of the book] where you have placed it—at the foot of the Cross."

In reply to the note of another teacher he wrote next day the subjoined answer, which needs some little explanation to make it intelligible.

A foolish, ruthless barbarian, regardless alike of gratitude, respect for age, and sympathy for sorrow, published a series of articles denouncing both the school and its Principal in no measured terms. The attack on himself might have been borne with equanimity, but to find fault with the Packer was to touch the very apple of his eye. And to make the cut still keener, the articles were signed " An Old Graduate." Sharp thrusts from outsiders might be borne with philosophical resignation, but that one who bore towards him and her Alma Mater the relation of a daughter should be guilty of such a cowardly act almost broke the sensitive, affectionate heart, and led him some months later to offer his resignation.

This is his note, probably in answer to one of sympathy from the person to whom it was written :

April 8, 1882.

DEAR MISS T——— :

Many thanks for your note of yesterday. How strange that these defects in character and attainment, like latent heat, should have been hid for so many years, all the more remarkable as I have been all these years in charge of a large institution that no one has considered a failure ! And most of all re-

markable as I have all the time been intimately associated with the most cultivated and refined people,
and during the time have received four honorary
diplomas.

As ever and truly your friend,

A. CRITTENDEN.

The recipient of the above has sent for insertion
in this memorial an exceedingly fair and critical
view of Dr. CRITTENDEN in his relation to female
education, written probably with a thought of the
above facts. Perhaps it will find no more fitting
place than this chapter :

" Dr. CRITTENDEN'S great strength as an educator was, I imagine, in his discernment of the
average demands of the community, and his con-
fining his efforts to supplying these rather than
seeking to bring them to an impossible or, for the
present, unattainable ideal.

" In this way he made the Packer a *popular*
school. An idealist would have elevated its
standard of scholarship, and would have done
better work for the smaller number of pupils who
would accept his views, but would not have carried the community with him. There is need for
both; the people must have what they will take

until they can be educated, by forces that are constantly at work enlarging and elevating the popular intelligence, to perceive and accept something higher.

"The daughters of the higher class of intellectual men will be educated in any case, more or less, by the atmosphere they live in. It may be a greater service to the community to provide the instruction which the commercial classes will appreciate.

"Dr. CRITTENDEN'S unimpeachable integrity and high standard of purity in social conduct are well worthy of mention."

The result of these public attacks was to cause the removal of a few pupils from the school; and the Principal, tired with his long journey, bowed down with his family sorrow, weakened by failing health, and disheartened by his apparent failure to secure the ends for which he had so long and faithfully labored, conceived the morbid idea that his removal would be advantageous to the school, and sent in his resignation to the Trustees in the following note:

To the Trustees of the Packer Collegiate Institute.

GENTLEMEN : In 1845 I accepted from your predecessors an invitation to take charge, as Principal, of
the institution of which you are the legal guardians.
I pledged my best efforts to co-operate with the Trustees to establish, and build up, an institution that
should be an ornament and a pride to this beautiful
city. In this work I have given, for more than a
generation of time, my best services, and I am satis-
fied with the results of our united efforts.

Time has passed so pleasantly and so silently that
I cannot realize that I have passed my threescore
and ten, the limit assigned to the best faculties of
body and mind; and while I am not conscious that
either are impaired, it is quite certain that they soon
will be, and it becomes my duty, though a painful
one, to resign, as I now do, my position as Principal.

No one of the Board who elected me to the honorable and responsible position I have occupied so
many years remains to receive my thanks for their
uniform courtesy and kindness.

You, as they, have imposed upon me obligations I
can never discharge. The best I have to give is my
heartfelt gratitude.

With perfect respect,

A. CRITTENDEN.

It is unnecessary to say that the proposition
embodied in the above letter was never for a
moment entertained by the Board of Trustees,
who at their next meeting unanimously passed
the following resolution:

April 24, 1884.

On motion of Judge Van Cott,

Resolved, That the resignation of Dr. CRITTENDEN be not accepted, and that the matter be referred to the President to confer with Dr. CRITTENDEN upon his communication.

Learning that his old and revered friend and colleague contemplated this step, Professor Eaton wrote him the following warm, loving letter:

PACKER COLLEGIATE INSTITUTE,
April 23, 1882.

MY DEAR FRIEND:

I desire to make one more effort to dissuade you from your purpose to resign your place at the head of this Institution.

I. There is no urgent necessity for such a course. You are certainly as well qualified for the duties of your position, both mentally and physically, as you have been for several years. You are even in better condition now than one year ago, when you entertained the same purpose.

II. I fear your resignation at this juncture will be misunderstood by many. Occurring so soon after the recent malicious attacks on this Institution by some of the New York papers, your action will seem to result from a pressure caused by those attacks. I should be sorry to have the authors of those articles comfort themselves with any such false notion.

III. The Packer Institute is your life-work. It is your achievement, and will be your lasting monu-

ment. It will carry your name down to posterity as
really as the name of Packer. To it you have given
your noblest efforts and the best part of your life. It
is what you have made it. Stand in your place,
therefore, and work on until Providence shall indicate
more plainly than at present the wisdom of your proposed action.

IV. I ask you to desist for reasons personal to myself. You have been to me a father, a brother, a
friend. More than any other man you have influenced
my life and character. I love you more than I can
express, and more than you will ever know. While
the step you propose will not, I trust, and certainly
on my part cannot interrupt our friendship, it will, in
form at least, sever one tie which has long bound us
in perfect harmony. Let us work on hand in hand
as we are, and let Providence settle these doubtful
questions. You may yet outlive me, and I must confess I should not be sorry to have it so.

Let us be content, and put a cheerful courage on.
If you wish any relief, either from care or responsibility, put upon me what you like, but don't leave me.

While I am sure the Trustees will not, under any
circumstances, allow you to sever your connection
entirely with this Institution, I greatly prefer that
you will remain exactly as you are. I can so arrange
my department by Miss E——'s assistance as to give
you all the time and help, by way of oversight or
other work that you may wish.

Lastly, I ask, as a personal favor to me, that if you
are still resolved to take this step, you will withhold
your resignation until September next.

Say nothing of your intention ; let your name go

into the catalogue as usual, and thus give the Institution the benefit and influence of your name for one
year at least.

I am sure this will be best for the school and best
for you. When the autumn comes we will talk this
matter over again, and you can then do what may
seem wise. Wait and see what the new year will
bring forth.

Sincerely your friend and brother,

D. G. EATON.

" Never can I forget," says the Professor, " the
manner in which that letter was received. Dr.
CRITTENDEN, trembling with excitement, sprang
up the stairs to the laboratory with the agility of
years ago, and, with eyes swimming in tears, threw
his arms round me and kissed me like a child."

The letter answered its purpose ; the advice
was taken: the resignation was not pressed, and
when ALONZO CRITTENDEN died he was still
Principal of the Packer Institute.

But sorrows more personal in their nature were
now pressing upon the sorrowing husband's heart.
The friend and companion of so many years
rested from her labors and sufferings May 5,
1882, and, as all around her had ample reason to
believe, "awoke in that likeness" of which she had

already exhibited so much. His sorrow, though deep and real, was manly and subdued rather than childish or sentimental. He accepted all the sympathy and consolation offered him, and cherished every scrap of writing which related to her.

A few extracts from these letters of condolence, which are after all really expressions of appreciation for himself, are given below. The following, written by his Greenville friend, was rather intended as a memorial than a letter:

"Another link is broken which has made the past so beautiful in many lives. The influence of a noble, true woman when associated from year to year with the young under her care cannot be estimated. The power that moves in the land is often silent, but trace back the growth of that strength and you find a little seed has taken root in one young heart many, many years ago. It did not die, but sprang up and bore fruit. It sowed itself again in other hearts and minds, and lo! the fruit returns a thousandfold. Nothing can arrest its wide-spread influence. It was 'sown beside all waters,' and year after year has increased and extended until many arise and call her blessed who wrought this great good.

"She whom we mourn, but for whom we ought to rejoice, and who has left us to enter upon her reward, was such a one. Strong, faithful, unswerving in the line of duty, she inspired the fainting heart, strengthened the weak, and by her example encouraged all high and laudable ambitions. A long life of earnest labor such as hers cannot close without calling forth a responsive throb in many hearts, and far, far away from her last resting-place the tear of love falls, and we mourn with those who are near that the loving words are all spoken, are all written, are all in the past.

"But for her we know there is rest. 'Blessed are the dead who die in the Lord. They rest from their labors, and their works do follow them.'

"From one who knew and loved her many years ago, and whose privilege it has been to enjoy a life-long friendship."

The following letter of condolence was at once sent to Dr. CRITTENDEN, and a copy of resolutions drawn up and adopted by the Board of Trustees which will be found in the Appendix:

May 1, 1882.

DEAR DR. CRITTENDEN :

Pray accept the assurance of our most cordial sympathy in this hour of sorrow. The loss can only be measured by the greatness of the blessing that has been enjoyed, and surely our gratitude is due to Him who has so long preserved that precious life,—restoring her soul when so often she seemed to be at the very entrance of the valley of the shadow, and leading her ever in the paths of righteousness.

May the God of all comfort and sustain you and have you in His holy keeping.

Truly your friends,

[Signed by twenty-eight lady teachers.]

The school was dismissed after morning prayers on the day of the funeral, and a large number of friends attended the services, which were held in the afternoon at Dr. CRITTENDEN'S residence next door to the Institute. Notices briefly mentioning the social and moral worth of the dead appeared in both Brooklyn and Albany papers.

The following are from the letters of condolence received during the weeks that followed:

1 SOUTH OXFORD STREET,
May 10, 1882.

Prof. Crittenden.

DEAR FRIEND: I was hoping to be at the sad obsequies of your beloved wife, but was hindered from coming. So I take this mode of expressing our deepest sympathy with you in this time of dire trouble. We have talked much of what must have been the grief of parting from one so long your companion and helpmate. It must be a consolation that the paths are divergent only for a short time, and that then they meet at the gate. From the infinite source of comfort may there pour consolation into your lacerated heart! My family join in the hope that you may be able to bear up under this domestic calamity. Commending you to God and the word of His grace, I am

Yours, etc.,
T. DE WITT TALMAGE.

RECTORY, ST. PAUL'S CHURCH,
TIVOLI-ON-HUDSON, N. Y.,
May 8, 1882.

DEAR FRIEND:

My daughter has just written me the sad intelligence of your grievous loss in life. To be deprived of a chosen, faithful, and beloved companion who for many years has journeyed with us is a calamity in almost any view. It brings in so great a change, it cuts off so many threads, it leaves the web of our future here with a ragged edge. And yet it is

God's will, and the discipline of His providence all the way along is to bring us to the recognition that His will is not only law but loving-kindness.

You know where to find consolation and support in your sore trial, and I pray that you may find all that you need and seek. In the Christian hope, with sympathy and regard, I remain

[Rev.] G. L. PLATT.

COLUMBUS, MISS.

I must tell you of the love and sympathy that fills our hearts for you whom our mother loved so tenderly.

I know not how it is with those who are looking on life's western slopes, but to us who have scarcely reached the hill-tops it is hard to realize we are in the hands of a kind and tender Father who doth not willingly afflict and yet *knows* how hard these trials are to bear. Yet faith, hope, and love all tell us God doth not leave His own. Our loved ones are not dead. They are the living.

Your friend, A. C. B.

In the spring of 1872 the Alumnæ Association formed at the close of the silver-wedding exercises, but so far existing only in name, was through the energy of some of its members resuscitated. Several meetings were held in the chapel, a con stitution was adopted, old graduates sought for, and a general social reunion arranged.

Dr. CRITTENDEN took great interest in all these proceedings notwithstanding the personal sorrows which were then gathering around his life, and he promised to be one of the few invited guests at the entertainment.

Before the appointed time, however—May 27th —Mrs. Crittenden had passed away, and her bereaved husband did not feel equal to the task of meeting so many old and sympathizing friends. Instead he sent the following letter, which was read at the dinner-table, those present responding by adopting resolutions of appreciation and sympathy :

May 26, 1882.

To the Alumnæ Association of the Packer Collegiate Institute.

MY DEAR CHILDREN : Accept my thanks for your cordial invitation to lunch with you on Saturday, the 27th inst.

Could I meet you, no one who encouraged me at the start would be there to congratulate me as I near the goal—no trustee, no teacher, no assistant of any kind whatever : all have joined the long procession and are on the other side.

Still you meet under circumstances of peculiar and, it seems to me, of intense interest.

You are the representatives of more than two generations of time, and of thousands who have shared with you the advantages of this Institution. A summary of what has been accomplished by your predecessors may not, at this time, be inappropriate or uninteresting to you.

Previous to the present century female education, relative to intellectual development, had received almost no attention either in this country or abroad.

In the early part of this century Mrs. Emma Willard, of blessed memory, did more than any other individual of her day to arouse the attention of the public to the importance of female education.

In 1811 Chancellor Kent, John V. Henry, Gideon Hawley, and others of like culture, residents of Albany, desiring facilities for the higher education of their own daughters, formed an association, erected a building, and commenced operations. In 1820 more commodious buildings were erected, and the association was incorporated under the name of the Albany Female Academy. The Legislature gave it a small endowment, the first money ever devoted by them to female education.

The late Chancellor Ferris of New York was for several years president of the Board of Trustees, and after his removal to the metropolis exerted his influence in founding a similar institution in that city, known as the Rutgers Female Institute, now Rutgers College.

In 1845 an institution formed under the same general plan was established in this city, and known as the Brooklyn Female Academy.

Other institutions of a like character followed in quick succession, all seeming to have a common origin ; so that you may consider yourselves as coming in a regular if not in an apostolic succession.

In 1850 the following report was made to the stockholders of the Brooklyn Female Academy : " The patronage of the Institution has far exceeded the most sanguine expectation of its friends, and in proof of this statement we are able to enumerate among the pupils who have sought the advantages of an education within its walls the representatives of nineteen different States of our Union, the Canadas, St. Thomas, Trinidad, Cuba, Sandwich Islands, and England."

In 1853 the building, with its library, chemical and astronomical apparatus, was destroyed by fire.

In September of 1854, through the patronage of one of your own number, we were more eligibly located in our present beautiful edifice, and surrounded with greater facilities to aid us in our work.

In 1871 the Alumnæ celebrated its twenty-fifth anniversary. Of the six hundred and four graduates, three hundred assembled in the chapel of the Institute. Reports of the different members of the classes from 1847 to 1871 were read, showing that many of them had become eminent as teachers, authors, missionaries, etc.

It certainly is a subject for gratitude and congratulation that while the world is circled with benign influences flowing from this Institution, no graduate, so far as I know, has ever disgraced herself or her Alma Mater. For nearly half a century the Packer Collegiate Institute has by common consent been acknowledged to be the leading institution in the State, if not in the country. Better endowed seminaries are opening all around us. What the future of our beloved and cherished Packer shall be depends very largely upon the society you represent.

With my best wishes for the health and happiness of you all—every one—I am, and ever shall be,

Your friend,   A. CRITTENDEN.

The following are the resolutions passed after the reading of the letter:

RESOLUTIONS.

Whereas, At a recent meeting of the Alumnæ of the Packer Institute, it was unanimously voted that a committee be appointed to draft resolutions testifying our esteem for the Principal of the Institution, our continued and undiminished confidence in him, and our abiding interest in the welfare of the school ; therefore,

Resolved, That we, the Alumnæ, desire to express formally our respect and affection for Dr. CRITTENDEN ; our appreciation of his life-long services in the cause of education, and of his devotion to the interests of the Packer-Institute ; and our sense of personal obligation to him for intellectual stimulus and moral inspiration.

Resolved, That we retain a warm interest in our Alma Mater, the influence of whose wise teachings and faithful guidance in the past will be with us always ; and that we fully confide in the helpful wisdom and ability of those associated with the Principal in the conduct of the school to assure its continuing and increasing usefulness in the future.

Resolved, That a copy of these resolutions be transmitted to Dr. CRITTENDEN, and also be recorded in the minutes of the Association.

E. B. McEWEN, *President.*
M. E. WINSLOW, *Vice-President.*
FANNY ELKINS, *Treasurer.*
M. C. LEFFINGWELL, *Secretary.*

CHAPTER X.

A GARNERED SHEAF.

The Professor's Illness—Death in the Home—Last Visit to Washington—Last Visit to the Packer—Fading Away—The End—Journalistic Eulogiums—The Last Obsequies.

DR. CRITTENDEN spent that last summer and autumn chiefly at his country home at Englewood; taking short trips in various directions, and making visits among his old Berkshire friends. His remaining brother, Alvan, was in a precarious state of health, and his solicitude for him is expressed in many of his home letters. He appears also to have been exceedingly anxious for the comfort of a nephew who was also in delicate health, and who he feared was not lodged with sufficient warmth and luxury to suit his enfeebled condition. In a letter written as autumn draws on he suggests extensive alterations to his nephew's house, and says they *can* be done; "if ten men cannot do the work, employ fifty;" and he adds, "Draw on me for money to pay the bill. Do this rather than suffer yourself and let your family." In a still later letter he writes, although in the midst of describing his own home sorrows :

"Don't send me my interest till you have got into your new house and have money to invest."

The summer's rest and change in some measure recuperated the old man's health and spirits, and when he took his accustomed place at the opening of the fall term there seemed to be no reason why he should not continue to occupy it for several' years longer. The Institution had been thoroughly renovated during the summer vacation; steam-heaters and the most approved ventilating apparatus introduced; the pupils at the opening were more numerous than ever, and all things gave promise of an exceedingly prosperous year.

The first shadow was Professor Eaton's illness. He had had one violent attack during the preceding spring, and being obliged to visit the city frequently in order to superintend the alterations through the summer, he had no chance of recuperation. Again and again during the autumn he was compelled to be absent from his duties for several days together, and at Thanksgiving time broke down entirely. By the advice of his physicians he was sent to the mountains of North Carolina, and has not since resumed his place.

So sensitive a nature as Dr. CRITTENDEN'S could not but feel this continued suffering of one so dear and so intimately associated with him very deeply, all the more as he realized his own incapacity for extra work.

Professor W. Le Conte Stevens was, on recommendation of Mr. Eaton, engaged to supply his place during his absence. He proved amply competent to perform all his duties, but still it was hard for the octogenarian who for almost sixty years had stood at the head of an institution to realize that its administration could glide along easily and successfully from day to day deprived of the supervision of one of its legitimate governors, and he felt anxious and troubled as the days passed by.

And now the home cares and sorrows multiplied, and the last shadows closed in.

On October 19th, Edward, the eldest grandson,

was attacked with diphtheria, and after eleven days' illness died, leaving sad hearts behind him, especially that of the grandfather, to whom he had been a child of great promise, and to whom, as he was now almost nine years old, he was an interesting companion. Dr. CRITTENDEN did not see Edward during his illness, as he still continued to attend to his duties in the Packer every day.

But in three weeks after the death of the eldest, little Margaret, the "precious pearl" to whom one of his letters was addressed, sickened with the same disease, and almost simultaneously it appeared in his granddaughter Bessie Dana, and two weeks latter little Alonzo—"Alonzo the brave," as his grandfather called him—had a similar though slight attack.

A general alarm was now felt throughout the school and the community, so many families of which were represented therein, and by advice of physicians Dr. CRITTENDEN ceased his daily attendance, and the other children were sent to a boarding-house, at which they remained for over a month. Their brother died October 30th, and was buried the 31st, on his ninth birthday.

In a letter dated November 20th the sad grandfather detailed these domestic sorrows to his nephew, adding :

" With the blessing of the good Father, we hope all will be well. He is too wise needlessly to afflict. Pray that we may have grace and faith to say, ' Thy will be done.' . . . Your uncle Alvan cannot last long : and then of a family of ten I am alone,—but only for a day."

A few days later he wrote to the same :

" We are all passing rapidly to the unseen country ; we cannot tell who will be called next. It is of no consequence if we are prepared. I had a violent attack of my old complaint, want of breath, last night, and it did not seem as though I should see the morning. These scenes of sickness and death have completely unnerved me, and one straw more will be too much for the camel's back."

Indeed, the gloom of the house, the loneliness to which his social nature was condemned, his sorrow for his grandchild, and the enforced separation from all his customary duties and interests, told very heavily upon a constitution enfeebled by age and sorrow. On one of the rare occasions when his daughter-in-law was able to leave her nursery cares and amid her own sorrows seek to lighten his, he told her he had never in his long life so thoroughly appreciated what it was to be lonely.

He had one attack of his old trouble—as he supposed—on November 14th, and another, mentioned above, on the 25th. The physicians afterwards concluded that both were connected with the heart-trouble of which he finally died.

It was therefore thought best that Dr. CRITTENDEN should accompany his old friend Professor Eaton as far as Washington on his Southern journey.

He was accompanied by his eldest granddaughter, and was quite interested in her enjoyment of this her first visit to the Nation's Capital.

From here he wrote the following letter to his two remaining grandsons. It is of great interest, as showing the wonderful elasticity of spirits and the perpetual spring of the ever-young heart which could thus in the midst of its own loneliness, weakness, and sorrow draw upon its unfailing resources to interest and amuse little children.

WASHINGTON, D.C., December 8, 1882.

My Dear Little Namesake and his Dimpled Brother.

MY YOUNG HEROES : You were noble boys to be so good and brave for nearly three weeks. I trust you both will be prepared to meet any other emergency with equal fortitude. We all did miss you so much : but it was harder for you than for us. How delightful it will be for us all to be together once more ! Yes ! all but dear grandma and dear Edward. They, we trust, are with the precious Saviour and with the angels, where there is no sickness, no death. Let us live in hope that we may by and by all be together where there is no sorrow.

I am quite confined to the house on account of this terribly cold weather. Kittie [his granddaughter] is out sight-seeing, and there is a great deal to see in Washington. This is a beautiful city, the capital of a great nation of over 50,000,000 people. The Capi*tol* was intended to be the centre of the Capi*tal*. How is this ? Ask mamma.

This building, the Capitol, covers six times as much ground as there is in the Packer grounds where you play. [Here follows a minute description of the Capitol and of other public buildings in Washington.]

But I cannot tell you anything more. I trust you will take a good look at all when one of you comes as the President and the other as Secretary of State.

[Here follow directions as to the care of the bulbs in the Institute garden, winter arrangements in the home, etc.]

It is so cold that I am forced to keep the house. Prof. Eaton is not quite so well.

God bless you all, every one. GRANDPA.

Shortly before the "holidays" the patriarch returned, and once more gathered his broken family around him. The reunion was sweet though sad, and some other relatives were invited to spend Christmas.

The daily letters which from the time of his return were either written or dictated to Professor Eaton, give so graphic a picture of the last days of the writer that we cannot resist the temptation to present our readers with copious extracts:

Sunday, December 10th.

We are at home again, the best place of all the world, and—thanks to a kind Providence—all together once more. Thank the Good Father with us. . . . I feel considerable of my short breath and a little faintness, indicating you know what. . . . Am in the right place. It was well, very well that we came home. . . . You are a poor wanderer, and you will not find the place you are looking for till you get back to Brooklyn—charming Brooklyn, full of friends and no enemies—not one.

December 11th.

It was a good thing for me to come home just at this time. All is well at the Packer, but it is time that some one should speak with more authority than a substitute. . . . T. M——'s eldest son is very sick; prayers in church were offered for him morning and evening. How much trouble the M——'s have had! I should think Mr. M—— would abandon the place. But sickness and death know no place. Thanks to God, there is a place where there are no sorrow, no sickness, no death.

December 16th.

Ever since I returned from Washington I have had premonitions of a return of my Lakewood trouble. This morning I arose at one o'clock, and am alive. The fact is, I did really think my days were not only numbered, as I still think, but from very fear took a carriage this morning and went to see Dr. Clark. Like a New England schoolmaster, he told me to take my coat off and went through me till he exclaimed, "Eureka!" He thinks it is the same old trouble, and he seems to think the same old medicine will relieve me. I trust I shall be able to keep my bed to-night till two o'clock. . . . When shall we find rest? One week more and the old year will give place to another, it may be of greater trials. Next Friday will be pay-day. Shall I deposit your check or send it to you?

December 23d.

Give my kind regards to ——, especially to Mr. and and Mrs. Randall, whom we met abroad and who were great favorites of Mrs. Crittenden, who is waiting on the other side for them and for us.

As "murder will out," I may as well tell you frankly

as to have you find it out in a roundabout way that I have not kept my word with you. I am sick and have to borrow K.'s hand to reply to your letter. Yesterday I sat up just long enough to have my bed made, and to-day I arose a little before twelve o'clock. Matters come on so well at the Institute that the conviction might be forced upon us that we are not nearly as important as we may have fancied. It might be true in one case, but it certainly would not be in the other.

Yesterday the machine closed for the year under a great clash of trumpets. The President, his Honor the Mayor, Judge Van Cott, Dr. Hall of the Holy Trinity, and others were present, and are said to have enjoyed it. I was in bed, and of course had a good time. . . . Mrs. Packer was greatly delighted, and when she is pleased all are pleased. During the day Mr. Low made me quite a long visit. I told him I had received several petitions that the holiday vacation should be prolonged one day. Of course he granted the petition.

On Christmas Day Dr. CRITTENDEN had another attack, differing slightly from those which had preceded it, which his family think was in the nature of paralysis, as ever after that time it seemed difficult for him to speak distinctly.

All through the week he continued to be very miserable, not rising in the morning till a late hour, though remaining with the family the rest of the day. His letters thus tell the history of the 'holiday" week:

December 29th.

Mrs. Eaton seems to be now as always doing the right thing at the right time. I don't mean in sending us flowers of such exquisite beauty and fragrance. The receipt of these has or should have been acknowledged, for they were exceedingly beautiful, and what seems to be peculiar was the continuance of their freshness and aroma. You must have breathed upon them before they were sent. By the bye, I thank you for reporting the state of the weather; it has quite relieved me from performing that sort of duty here, as I observe from day to day that your thermometer corresponds with ours. Did you not make a mistake and take one of ours with you? The young Professor is sitting by and smiles a little incredulously at the suggestion, thinking perhaps it may not account for the phenomenon. He is a little puzzled to reconcile my solution of the fact that your barometer makes the weight of the air very different from ours. I, however, account for it from the desire I know you to have, very pre-eminently, to rise in the world. The young Professor says there is one barometer you have certainly carried with you—a plucky spirit—and that keeps you mounted on an elevation that indicates a certainty of your surmounting all present troubles.

You must value this letter especially from the circumstances under which it is written. K. is acting as amanuensis; I am in bed dictating; Professor S. is on the other side laughing at the nonsense; B. is at the foot of the bed, wondering that grandpa being so old and sick should be so foolish.

January 1, 1883.

You certainly know without being told that this is a New Year, bright and beautiful and fresh as though it was the first day of the first one that ever lighted up this glorious earth. No clouds above, no fogs below, perfect temperature, and heart-greetings from all sides. St. Ann's chimes rang out the old and rang in the new, and now all seems to be ready for warm congratulations; at any rate I am, in the middle of my large bed on my back, dictating a letter to our loved absent ones. . . . How I wish we could see you and give you a New Year's greeting! Let us hope that at no distant future we may meet face to face and thank the Lord for His tender mercy and loving-kindness. . . .

We are surrounded by a vast many things to cheer us. In spite of all, however, the memories of the last year throw a very deep shadow all around us; but for these I think I could say with Mr. B. after the loss of his wife, "Till now life has been a poem."

I know that I should feel that all the past, however fraught with all that this life can give, is not to be compared with those scenes which no eye hath seen, no ear hath heard, neither hath it entered into the heart of man to conceive, and which are reserved for those that love Him. May I not feel that I have your prayers that all these mists which obscure the future may pass away?

On the morning of January 3d, to the great surprise of all, he rose early, dressed, and came down to breakfast, announcing his intention of being present at morning prayers the opening day of school for the new year.

In vain his daughter and niece both endeavored to dissuade him; and the latter, seeing he was resolved upon the hazardous experiment, sent for Mr. Low, who carefully assisted his old friend down the steps and along the few yards of pavement which lay between his home and the Institute. He was terribly exhausted with the climb up the many stairs to the chapel, and when there was hardly able to speak. However, he read in a tremulous voice from the 17th to the 27th verse of John, 17th chapter, sitting meanwhile in an arm-chair and uttering a few words of New Year's greeting.

The service, which to most of those present was one of painful interest, was soon over, and kind hands were ready at once to assist the honored Principal back to his home. He made no resistance: perhaps he felt, in spite of his natural elasticity, that he had stood in his old place for the last time.

His audience did not think so; but now they are glad to remember that the last time he walked from his own door it should have been to the accustomed place of duty which he had visited almost daily for over thirty years. He never went out again; he only appeared in the chapel once more: but that time he was carried reverently up the long staircases and laid gently beneath golden sheaves of ripened grain, surrounded as he had loved to be by young and friendly faces, while the words of prayer from the desk above his upturned face were spoken by other lips than his.

The following is his own account of that last chapel service.

January 3d.

I have just come in from the chapel. In going over I encountered various obstacles — formidable ones. Rank No. 1, plucky little Mary [his niece]; then came Margaret and Fanny. Mr. Low met me in the hall, gave me his arm and a cordial New Year's greeting. They were just ready to read the Scriptures. The school was well represented. I gave the scholars my own and your congratulations, told them I had felt constrained to reject their application for an extra day, but had referred it not to a kinder but to a more generous heart, and that I was happy to see that they had not abused the indulgence. Mr. Low made a very appropriate and timely address, and then gave me his arm again and said he was going to see me home.

During the next day Dr. CRITTENDEN remained in bed, "not," he says in his daily bulletin to Mr. Eaton, " that there is any particular reason for it, for I am as well as yesterday, and better, but it is an easy way to spend the morning and the only way to keep my nieces in anything like good humor."

The next, January 5th, he wrote: " I did not go to the chapel this morning, though I am stronger and better able than yesterday: but yesterday was New Year's and to-day is not. I am certainly better than yesterday, though I must confess to you I feel miserable to-day."

Later his niece, who acted as his amanuensis, added the following postscript to the letter:

" Uncle has felt very faint all the morning, owing, I think, to his dressing, shaving, and coming downstairs before breakfast. The doctor is coming to-day, and I shall ask him about it. Uncle is one of the men, as you know, who does not learn from experience regarding his strength. If we could only make him careful, I think he could get as well as he was last summer; but he is very feeble and requires the greatest care."

On the 6th he wrote: " I cannot bear the least fatigue; I don't believe I could write a letter of four pages to save my life."

On the morning of January 3d ALONZO CRIT-TENDEN'S life-work closed, and during the twenty days which remained he was rapidly drifting towards the end. His mind was clear till almost the last, as was evidenced by the daily letters which he either wrote or dictated to his friend and colleague Professor Eaton:

January 9th.

Though I am comfortable to-day, I am almost at the giving-up point. I am sorry to tell you all this, but I was resolved to let you know the facts as they really exist. As I have contemplated the prospect of leaving the dear ones dependent upon me, I have felt exceed-ingly anxious to consult you once more. If we both get better I may wish to write you confidentially. In the mean time it is our duty to place ourselves entirely in the hands of the loving Father and say, " Thy will be done."

He made his business arrangements calmly and with his usual judgment; he received and greatly enjoyed the visits of his friends; he even wrote a note to his old friend Mrs. D., thanking her for a call which he had greatly enjoyed. He sent for

some friends and former pupils whom he had not
seen for some time, talked with them earnestly,
and bade them an affectionate good-by.   He
spoke of his " decease which he should accomplish"
with perfect fearlessness; for what has he who
has trusted his Saviour for over sixty years to do
with fear when that Saviour at last sends the summons to " come up higher" ?

About the middle of January Professor Eaton
became alarmingly ill.   Dr. CRITTENDEN was
greatly distressed not only at his friend's condition, but also at his own inability to go to his bed-
side.   He at once dictated the following :

January 10th. 'l

M. has just read me your letter of January 7th, and
I am very greatly distressed.   In my last letter I told
you frankly and fully what seemed to be my true condition, and I am exceedingly glad that you tell me now
the worst of yours. . . . I am rejoiced to know that
you feel safe in the arms of the blessed Father and
are at peace,   It is our daily prayer that the blessed
Lord who scourgeth every son whom He receiveth may
soon restore you to health and to your position of
usefulness.

. . . If I were well, you would see me on the arrival
of the next express.

On the 11th he sent a telegram to Asheville with the words, "How is Professor Eaton? Whom shall I send to you?" and followed it with a note in which he offered to send some one on.

" You need," he says, "some one with you, and I want you to say which one of your friends it shall be. We are all with you in spirit, but you ought to have some one in bodily presence."

The niece who watched over him so tenderly said that her uncle, although gradually gaining, had been thrown back again by his anxiety for his associate; but he still thought himself growing better, and wrote on the 12th, "I am gaining at the rate of ten knots an hour, and expect to be at school on Monday provided I can get a good night's sleep."

Even while dictating these words the sick man was so weak that he dropped asleep several times, and in a few days his hope of again resuming his place faded away. And the next day he wrote: "I am constrained to say that I am on my back, with no prospect that I can see of ever being at my work again."

A temporary improvement in the condition of

the absent invalid called forth the two following notes:

January 13th.

Cheer after cheer! Both telegrams received. How much better it is than waiting three days for a letter! Only now write in the major key every time. . . . The days come and go, with me at least, in a most sad monotony. We had a little variety last night in calling Dr. Speir at three o'clock. I really gave the people a little fright. Not so, however, the doctor. As a matter of taste I have kept my bed until this moment, 3.15 P.M., and I am now dictating my daily letters, which with others of the same class might better be termed *weakly*.

January 14th.

We have another Sabbath; and though the earth is wrapped in clouds, I trust the sky above them is clear and beautiful to your eyes of faith and peaceful trust. The last night has been to me one of great suffering, but I am better this morning, and I hope to hear that you are a great deal better. . . . How I wish I could see you, if but for an hour!

The last clear intelligible letter which Dr. CRITTENDEN dictated bears the date of January 16th. It is full of business details and wise advice, and closes with the following:

January 16th.

Yesterday was a very arduous, solemn, and thoughtful day. I found it necessary from various circumstances to review my will, and I need not tell you it

cost me an effort for which I found myself illy prepared. But it is done, and I trust finally—not exactly
satisfactorily. . . . Your accounts are just as mine are
not, always in order, and so send for your rents at any
time. . . . The cheerful accounts received from yourselves and your physician in relation to your health
have spread a silver lining over the whole atmosphere.
See that you keep it (the lining) bright. The exam-
inations in physical sciences under the young Professor have just closed. I have not received reports of
the success except from K., who passed ninety-two
and is much delighted.

"A sudden pull up," as Weller would say.

As always,

A. CRITTENDEN.

One more attempt was made January 17th, but
it is a little flighty; the ready writer made one
more illegible attempt to write with his own hand,
and then laid down his pen, and the daily bulletins
were thenceforth dictated by another brain.

Professor Stevens, in the exquisite little sketch
which he has contributed for this volume, has
drawn a picture of these sunset hours, which his
faithful and devoted kindness and attention amply
qualified him to do. Other friends have testified
of the brightness of that sick-room, but they are
the nearest and the dearest, and their reminiscences are too sacred to appear in print.

In spite of the weakness and prostration of that
first school-morning of the year, and in spite of the
frequent attacks of pain, difficult breathing, and
faintness—chronicled in these letters—the sick man
lingered on until almost the end of the month, ral-
lying so much at times that some hopes were entertained of his temporary recovery. He in-
structed his son to bid good-by to his associates
in the Packer, and continued to express great
anxiety concerning Professor Eaton's condition.
But a few days before January 23d he had another
attack of partial paralysis, which rendered the
meaning of all he said from that time exceedingly
doubtful.

Dr. CRITTENDEN was a little delirious at times
for a week before his death, but insisted upon get-
ting up each day and being dressed. On Monday,
the day before he died, he walked unaided into his
daughter's room, and even started to go downstairs, apparently, however, changing his plan in
order to make a last arrangement for the comfort
of the dear ones he was leaving behind. And this
is a touching instance of his life-long habit of
caring for and arranging for others, strong in

almost the very hour of death. Turning from the stairs, he feebly tottered into the little room at the end of the hall, which he used as a study. Here he had a fearful fit of exhaustion ; and when he had in some degree recovered, managed to say to his son, in broken words and sentences, that ready money would be needed by the family before his will could be acted upon, and that to save trouble and embarrassment he wished to put his signature to a check.

His son endeavored to put him off with the as-surance that there was money enough on hand, etc. But ALONZO CRITTENDEN had been for seventy years in the habit of having his wishes attended to and his purposes carried out. He seemed so distressed that Mr. Edward Crittenden procured a paper and proceeded to write out the form of a draft.

When it was finished, the trembling hand was reached out for paper and pen to sign the name for the last time. The A was distinct and charac-teristic; so was the C, with its sweeping curve below the line, so familiar to all who have seen it at the end of notes or on diplomas ; but then the letters began to run together, and the pen dropped from the trembling fingers, which were never again to resume it; for it is not to the glorified ones of his new abode that the command was given, "*Write.*"

"Just before the last," writes the daughter who watched so affectionately over him, "when his speech was so indistinct that we could scarcely understand him, he tried to repeat that beautiful hymn,

> "'Just as I am, without one plea,
> But that Thy blood was shed for me.'

I understood a word or two, and, repeating the hymn, said, 'Father, is that what you wanted to say?' and he smiled and nodded his head."

"Blessed are the dead who die in the Lord. Even so, saith the Spirit; for they rest from their labors; and their works do follow them."

ALONZO CRITTENDEN rested from his labors January 23d. His works are still following him.

The Brooklyn *Daily Eagle* of Tuesday evening, January 23, 1884, contained an editorial of which the opening sentence was, "Brooklyn has lost a valuable citizen and a successful educator by the death of Professor CRITTENDEN." A long eulogium of the teacher's profession followed, with the words, "Honor to the educators of America. They are more than statesmen. They make the men and women who make the homes which make the land. Their reward is not in 'storied urn or animated bust,' in long obituary or Latin epitaph, but in the grateful memories of those whom they have taught and who under their patient teaching have ceased to do evil and learned to do well. It is no mere obituary sentiment to say that the grief felt for Dr. CRITTENDEN'S death in hundreds of Brooklyn homes to-day is sincere, and that many an old pupil of his will shed a grateful tear upon the memory of what he did for them."

The same paper contained an announcement of the death, which occurred at a quarter before seven that morning, with a sketch of his life and public services, correct in the main. The *Tribune, Times, World, Sun,* and *Herald,* of New

York, and several Albany papers contained similar notices.

The U. S. flags on the City Hall and other public buildings were also lowered to half-mast —a great honor to be shown to a private citizen.

The pupils and teachers were informed of the death of their Principal, at the morning opening exercises, by Mr. A. A. Low, President of the Board of Trustees, after which the school was dismissed. The announcement was unexpected and the end seemed to have come suddenly, although their old friend had been ill so long, and the girls went away silently and in tears.   In the evening a special meeting of the Trustees was held in the library to take action regarding the death of the Principal and make arrangements concerning the funeral ceremonies.   Mr. Low called the meeting to order and spoke in feeling and eulogistic terms of the long, honorable, and useful career of the deceased. A minute and resolution were then presented by Judge J. M. Van Cott, which were unanimously adopted by the Board.   They will be found in the Appendix.

The next morning a memorial meeting, largely attended by both scholars and friends, was held in the chapel. The chair and desk for so many years occupied by the Principal were heavily draped with mourning. In front was a sheaf of golden wheat tied together with violets; this design being suggested and arranged by the graduating class. Mr. Low conducted the services and Professor S. Lazar directed the music. After the usual processional hymn sung by the school, Mr. Low read the same Scripture selections which Mr. CRITTENDEN had read on the morning of January 3d. The hymn "Paradise" followed, with prayer by Rev. Dr. Lansing,—one of the oldest and most constant friends of the Institution and its head, and since gone to join his old friend. The announcement of the funeral to be held in the chapel on Friday afternoon was read with the minute of the Board, and the hymn "Jerusalem the Golden" sung, after which the scholars were dismissed until the following Monday.

At the close of the exercises the Faculty and teachers of the Institution held a meeting and adopted a preamble and resolutions expressive of

sorrow, resignation, and sympathy with the bereaved family in this common affliction.

A special meeting of the Associate Alumnæ was
held in the laboratory in the afternoon, at which
Mrs. M. A. S. Kitchell presided. There was an
unusually large attendance, which was especially
marked as the notice was necessarily so short. It
was decided that the members of the Association,
and all other old graduates who desired to do
so, should attend the funeral in a body, wearing
mourning badges. A series of resolutions was
then adopted.

Similar meetings were held at the Polytechnic
Institute and Adelphi Academy, and at each a copy
of resolutions was adopted and a committee appointed to attend the funeral and represent the
Institution.

On Friday afternoon of January 26th the chapel
of the Packer was filled with a mournful assemblage, all anxious to pay a last tribute of respect to
one so widely known in the community and so intimately associated with much of its family life
In consequence of the limited accommodations the
younger departments of the school had been ex-

cused from attendance, but seats on the left of the platform and organ were reserved for the Collegiate and first and second Academic Departments, containing perhaps two hundred girls, to whom, under the direction of Professor Lazar, was committed the charge of the music.

Two hundred of the Alumnæ were seated in the gallery to the left, while on the side of the platform nearest them seats were reserved for the Trustees. The mourning drapery still remained, and several beautiful floral gifts were added by the teachers, scholars, and alumnæ.

At almost the same hour as that at which on Friday afternoons he had so many years sat on the platform and watched the long files of girls as they came into the chapel for the weekly reading of compositions, we sat and watched the procession of ministers and pall-bearers, who comprised the whole Board of Trustees, as they reverently bore to the platform the silent form of the Principal and laid it just where the afternoon sunshine slanting through the western window had so often fallen upon the young heads to whose crude effusions he had lent such indulgent attention.

We could not but feel that it was just what he would have desired, and that we had his pleased appreciation of all that we did.

The upturned face, visible in its uncovered coffin, surmounted by soft hair in which eighty-two winters had sowed only a few threads of silver, looked thin and showed marks of both mental and bodily suffering, but the expression was one of peace, and it seemed as though the still lips *must* open to give directions or take some part in the exercises.

The Rev. Dr. Storrs, Dr. CRITTENDEN'S pastor, conducted the services, read the Scriptures, and made the principal address; the Rev. Dr. H. M. Booth of Englewood, Dr. CRITTENDEN'S summer home, spoke also and very eloquently concerning the early years of his friend, and his unswerving fidelity to Christianity.   The Rev. Dr. S. I. Prime, senior editor of the New York *Observer*, offered the closing prayer.

The hymns sung by the young ladies were from the *Chapel Hymnal* compiled by Professor Lazar, and dedicated to "ALONZO CRITTENDEN, A.M., Ph.D." They were all his special favorites:

"Rock of Ages," "Just as I Am," "My Faith looks up to Thee," and "Abide with Me."

After the close of the last hymn the personal friends and family took leave of their dead, and then the scholars and alumnæ one by one passed round the coffin and took a last look at the familiar face and form which had been such an important factor in so many of their lives. It was quite sunset now, and it took very little exercise of imagination to fancy we could hear the familiar voice "far up the height" saying, as so often before, "Culture, character, happiness, success, heaven itself, is offered to your *acquisition*, not *acceptance*."

APPENDIX.

I.

Tributes to the Character of the late Professor Crittenden.

MANY tributes to Dr. CRITTENDEN'S character, abilities, and success have been sent to the writer of this memorial. Where they bore directly upon the story as it was being told, they have been incorporated in the body of the work. Others seemed either more complete in themselves or more general in their nature, and these she has thought best to group together.

By Dr. S. I. Prime, of the *New York Observer.*

The Rev. S. Irenæus Prime, D.D., was a lifetime
friend of Mr. CRITTENDEN, and was one of those
who took part in the funeral services. In a letter
to the editor of this volume Dr. Prime says:

"Of all the men with whom I have been intimately acquainted, I do not now remember
one who was more useful and successful as a
teacher of young women. There was a charm in
his manner that fascinated and inspired, so that
his pupils were not only delighted with their
study, but stimulated to their highest capacity
in the pursuit of knowledge. It was a real pleasure to me to be called in to the examination of
his classes in mental science, and to notice at once
the proficiency of the pupils who had fairly
grasped the subjects and were able to impart an
intelligent view to others, and also to observe the
extreme desire of the Professor to help the halting
young lady and enable her to present the best
possible appearance before the committee.

"Such was the kindliness of his nature that he
won the hearts while he was guiding the minds of
those who sat at his feet.

"I have been with him in festal seasons, when
marriage-bells made the home merry and his
heart was full of gladness: and again and again
when death darkened the house and sorrow filled

all hearts.   In every circumstance, he was the
same trustful, hoping, loving Christian friend.
We shall not see the like of him again.   He de-
serves to be held in memory and honor as one of
the most accomplished and successful educators
of our country and age.   And it is good to know
that such influences as he exerted will not die with
him nor with his pupils, but by them will be transmitted to generations yet to be.

"SAMUEL IRENÆUS PRIME."

By Professor W. L. Stevens of the Packer
Collegiate Institute.

In giving my brief tribute to the memory of Dr.
Crittenden it is due at the outset to remark that
my acquaintance with him began just as he was
about to leave forever the scenes with which his
life was identified. Three months after our first
meeting, the grave was opened and the aged
worker was consigned to rest.

In October, 1882, I was called upon to assume
the duties in Packer Institute which had been performed by one who for thirty years was the associate and warm personal friend of Dr. Crittenden. I had known each of these men
only by reputation. Involuntarily we form
mental pictures of those whom we have never
seen, and often the feeling is that of disappointment when we come into contact with the living
man and throw aside the ideal. I had heard
of Dr. Crittenden as one who had spent nearly threescore years in the actual work of education; and I expected to see a tottering old man,
white-headed, stern, opinionated, and more or less
saturated with the dogmatism that too often grows
out of long-continued rule. On meeting him there
was indeed disappointment, but it was of a pleasant
kind. I was introduced to one who seemed to be
not over sixty years of age, with but few gray

hairs, kind and genial in manner, lively and companionable, quick at repartee, evidently fond of young society, and in some respects younger in spirit than myself. His greeting was cordial, and at once I received evidence of his wish that I should be not merely an associate but also a friend.

These first impressions were conveyed despite the fact that Dr. CRITTENDEN's life had been but recently clouded with a great domestic sorrow in the loss of his wife. When conversation ceased his face assumed a perceptibly sad expression, but this was dispelled as soon as the interests of the moment suggested interchange of thought. It was evidently not natural to him, but only the product of recent affliction. He was indeed then passing through an ordeal of sorrow. The angel of death was again hovering over the stricken household, and two days after my arrival my new-found friend came to me to announce the death of his grandchild, a noble boy whom he loved with all the tenderness of his affectionate nature. He sought sympathy as naturally as he gave it. The experience of fourscore years had not made him any more self-sufficient, any more independent of fellow-feeling in joy or sorrow, than in the days of youth when the emotions are apt to surge in warmth. On the contrary, his emotional nature seemed to have been cultivated as well as disciplined. In committing to the dust all that remained of his favorite grandson, he grieved almost like a mother at the loss of her only child.

It was but a few weeks after this occurrence that

Dr. CRITTENDEN began to be confined to his room by the illness which terminated his life. Of him as a teacher and an administrator I can therefore say little. There are others who will do him justice in these relations. His failing health made it impossible to assume active duty, and my acquaintance was only with him as the aged pilgrim approaching the goal which he knew to be not far away. Even at the beginning of his illness he seemed convinced that the end was near at hand, and he faced it with calmness and resignation, though life had not lost its attractions. My visits to the sick-chamber were frequent, and his inquiries always showed that, even if his days were almost numbered, his active interest in the welfare of the Packer Institute should never flag. His native elasticity of spirit made him cheerful and companionable whenever friends could be admitted; and occasionally he seemed even to indulge the hope of recovery.

Throughout this illness the characteristics of Dr. CRITTENDEN which most impressed me were his tenderness of heart, his refined gentleness, his fidelity to the Packer and all that was connected with it. Other qualities he possessed in a marked degree, qualities which fitted him for conflict with the world; but perhaps those which are most naturally elicited in the sacred home-circle became emphasized, now that the world was fading away and conflict was at an end. On the eve of the Christmas holidays it was a sore trial to him to be unable to attend chapel exercises and give to the students the words of cheer and good-will that the season suggested. In performing this duty for him I obeyed his injunction, and gave his promise that at their first gathering in January he should be present to offer the greetings of the new year. The promise was fulfilled. Though really too weak to leave his chamber with prudence, he was assisted upstairs ; and for the last time he occupied an arm-chair in the chapel where morning after morning for over a quarter of a century he had led in the devotional exercises of prayer and praise to the God whom he had served, and to whose service he had helped to consecrate thousands of young women now scattered over the breadth of our land. The emotions stirred up by the occasion made it impossible for him to address the students ; but his mute presence told what none could have the heart to say. His tottering footsteps as he walked down the aisle, his haggard face, his feeble, trembling voice, all indicated that his last prayer in that chapel had been offered, his last words of greeting and counsel had been said. Hundreds of eyes were wet with tears, hundreds of voices quivered in song. The new year had dawned in gloom ; and, ere its first month closed, the arm-chair was taken away, and in its place stood a coffin upon which rested a sheaf of full ripe wheat.

That Dr. CRITTENDEN should have been uncommonly successful as a director in female education is not surprising. Rarely have I come into contact with any one who impressed me so much during a brief acquaintance. His success was largely due to his exquisite tact, ready sympathy, kindly geniality, and great quickness in reading human character. My memories of him are pleasant. exclusively pleasant; and in following him to his grave I felt that I had lost a friend who, if newly acquired, was none the less a friend indeed whom I could honor, trust, and warmly esteem.

W. LeConte Stevens.

By Professor C. E. West.

My Dear Miss W * * * *

I thank you for your kind invitation to aid in
the preparation of a memoir of Mr. CRITTENDEN,
late Principal of Packer Institute, which the Trustees of that Institution have wisely entrusted to
your hands. I am happy to comply with your re-
quest, and add my mite to the undertaking in the
form of a letter.

ALONZO CRITTENDEN has been identified with
the cause of education in this State for nearly sixty
years. In thousands of families his name is a
household word, as sacred and familiar as that of
father. Thousands of his pupils have felt the benign and subtle influence of his guiding mind. He
has reared an imperishable monument in the affections and memories of multitudes who venerate
his character.

My object in this communication will be briefly
to sketch my own impressions of his life and character.

Our acquaintance began more than fifty years
ago. We were born in adjoining towns in Massachusetts. Our families were intimately acquainted
and distantly related by marriage. Mr. CRITTEN-
DEN was my senior; and as boys we attended different academies, but completed our collegiate education at the same institution. He graduated in

1824, and was called to the Albany Female Academy to take part in its instruction, and was afterwards placed in charge of the institution as principal. It was there I met him. In 1833 I went to Albany to study law, but was soon drawn away from my intended purpose to engage in teaching boys. Our schools were near each other, and our intercourse was more or less intimate.

Albany was then the great political centre of the State. The Albany Regency was in the heyday of its popularity and power. It controlled the politics of the State. The society of the capital was brilliant and aristocratic. The Clintons, the Van Rensselaers, the Van Vectens, the Schuylers, the Spencers, the Van Burens, the Kents, and the Pruyns were among the distinguished families. It was the old Dutch city of colonial fame. It was noted for its distinguished men. Among its pulpit orators were William B. Sprague, John N. Campbell, B. T. Welsh, and Edwin N. Kirk. The legal and medical professions stood in the first rank; there were literary and scientific circles of no mean order. There Henry James, Sr., spent his early manhood in the city of his birth; Alfred B. Street sang his lovely pastorals; Anne C. Botta began to lisp in song; there Amos Dean wrote his History of Civilization; Chancellor Kent, the first President of the Academy, his Commentaries; Solomon Southwick, his Letters of a Layman; T. Romeyn Beck, his great work on Medical Jurisprudence; and Joseph Henry began his eminent scientific career. There John Paterson, the printer, read for his pastime the mathematical treatises of La Place and La Grange. The press was represented by such men as Edwin Croswell and Thurlow Weed. At an earlier day there might have been seen at the Tontine Coffee-House on State Street, a celebrated rendezvous, many of the leading politicians and distinguished men of the State. Among these were De Witt Clinton, Alexander Hamilton, Aaron Burr, Morgan Lewis, Daniel D. Tompkins, Chancellor Livingston, and many others.

It was in this small community of brilliant and cultivated people that Mr. CRITTENDEN began his life-work as a teacher. There was everything to stimulate the young man. The very atmosphere was surcharged with magnetic influences. There was no such thing as concealment from the eye of criticism. His work would be known and read of all men.

The Academy, founded in 1814, had gained nothing more than a local reputation. The buildings were poor and located in an undesirable part of the city; the patronage was small. Now was the time for action. Mr. CRITTENDEN took society as he found it, became a skilled tactician, and turned the current of popular influence to his advantage. This was right, so long as he did not violate the principles of comity and fair dealing. Success is often the cause of envy and disparagement, and sometimes of bitter hatred, in the heated rivalries of practical life. Mr. CRITTENDEN, while a wise and sagacious manager, had the reputation of being an honest man. No stain was ever found upon his moral character. He was a great ad- mirer of Dr. Nott, his college president. The Doctor was an eminent tactician, and in his lectures on Kames' 'Elements of Criticism' taught his stu- dents the great lessons of how to make the most of life. Many of his students became eminent poli- ticians, among whom were William H. Seward and John C. Spencer.

The Academy, as I have said, was founded in 1814, and was known as the Union School. In 1821 an act of incorporation was obtained from the leg- islature, and Chancellor Kent was chosen president of the board of directors named in the charter. The institution took its new corporate name of the Albany Female Academy. Mr. CRITTENDEN was the fourth principal. His predecessors were Hor- ace Goodrich, Tibbeus Booth, and Frederick Mat- thews. In the beginning the school was small— some thirty pupils. In 1821 a new spacious build- ing was reared, and so rapidly did the school in crease that an additional building was erected in 1827. These edifices continued to be occupied by the Academy till 1834, when its celebrity and num- bers became so great as to justify and demand the erection of a beautiful and commodious structure on one of the most fashionable streets of the city. A new career of prosperity opened before it. It be- came the pride of the city, and was patronized by the *élite* of society. Its anniversary exercises at- tracted large assemblies of admiring friends. It was a great success. For twenty years Mr. CRIT-

TENDEN presided over its fortunes, until he was called to this city to enter upon a greater work. His life in this city I leave to your own pen to describe. In passing, I wish to put upon record a little matter of personal history.

The first inception of the Brooklyn Female Academy may be found in the following note:

BROOKLYN, 29th October, 1844.

Charles E. West, Esq.

DEAR SIR: There are a number of persons in Brooklyn desirous of having a school here after the model of the Rutgers Female Institute. You would oblige me if you could, at some time convenient to yourself, give me the plan of that school as at first gotten up, with cost of buildings, yearly expenses, revenue, and any information relative thereto which it may be proper to impart; together with any suggestions which you might deem useful in organizing a similar institution.

Yours respectfully.
D. G. CARTWRIGHT.

I responded by inviting Mr. Cartwright and his friends to meet me at Rutgers Institute. He came in company with Mr. Francis Spies, and we talked over the course to be taken to awaken public interest in such an enterprise. We had several meetings which resulted in calling a public meeting in Brooklyn, notices of which were posted at the ferries and other places. A full attendance was had, the object was stated, a discussion followed, a subscription of stock was circulated, the amount proposed was secured, a board of trustees chosen, and a charter obtained. I planned the Academy building which was burned in the winter of 1852, and assisted in selecting a site and preparing a curriculum of the course of study. Mr. Cartwright was appointed trustee. He was an efficient worker and contributed much to the early success of the enterprise. He was pleased in witnessing the material realization of his ideal institution. Mr. CRITTENDEN was chosen principal, and his long service in the Institute has been a credit to himself and an honor to the city.

I came to Brooklyn in 1860, and for nearly a quarter of a century it has been my good fortune to live near him on terms of friendly intercourse. Although engaged in the management of independent institutions, we felt that we were laboring in a common cause for the benefit of the young. The field we were called upon to cultivate was large enough for both, with room to spare.

His home was the true ideal of a Christian household. His wife was an accomplished lady, and contributed largely to her husband's success. At the time of their marriage she was a young lady of rare personal beauty and refinement. I remember seeing her on their wedding-trip to her husband's native town. Her favorite exercise was horseback riding. Mounted on her spirited charger, she was queen of the turf. The impression she made on my youthful mind by those equestrian excursions has never faded. At the head of a large family of young ladies, she made her influence felt in moulding their manners and fitting them for the duties

and honors of society.   In old age she was lovely.
The mellowing tints of autumn came slowly on and
lent a charm to her classic face.   As her sun went
down, the shadows of earth grew longer and
darker but the heavens above which were to receive her spirit glowed with a divine beauty.

In forming an estimate of Mr. CRITTENDEN'S
character, it is not difficult to name its leading characteristics.   Among these, if I mistake not, were
intuitive insight, tact, push, industry, kindness, and
veneration.   He was quick to see, wise in the selection of means, and ready to act.   He was kind,
easily approached, vigilant, self-reliant, and untiring.   He venerated the great and good men of every
age.   He was conservative in religion and faithful to
every trust.   Such a man was sure to win his way
in the world, in whatever calling he chose.   He
was rewarded with a long career of usefulness.
He had reached the outer limit of human life before
the messenger came and summoned him to another
sphere of higher honors and more precious rewards.
The death of the good man brought grief to many
hearts and tears to many eyes.   There is consolation in the thought of such a loss, and that is, his
work did not die with him.   That abides.   The
rich harvest has been gathered for immortality.

CHAS. E. WEST.

BROOKLYN HEIGHTS SEMINARY, Oct. 15, 1884.

II.

Funeral Addresses.

DR. BOOTH'S ADDRESS.

ENGLEWOOD, N. J., Oct. 18, 1884.

MY DEAR SIR:

I send you a manuscript which contains so much of the address delivered at your father's funeral as I have been able to recall. Perhaps it may be of service to you. At all events, I shall be glad to drop a flower, however simple and common it may seem, upon his grave.

Sincerely yours,

HENRY M. BOOTH.

E. W. CRITTENDEN, Esq.

The shock of corn which the hand of affection has placed upon his bier is emblematic of the honored teacher's life. In it we read the lessons of his usefulness. For this is the harvest of many plantings, the ripe grain of a successful husbandry. By the fruits of the earth, which are gathered in their seasons, are represented industry, frugality, and intelligence. These are not the accidents of nature, nor are they to be referred alone to the operation of nature's laws. Man's thought and effort must be recognized, inasmuch as he has carefully preserved seed each year for the sowing, and has then cultivated the earth diligently in order that he may reap; and God's fidelity to the ancient covenant must also be recognized, since

He alone with the sunshine and the rain can give the increase.

No life of man stands apart from its environment or beyond the reach of the divine blessing. We owe much of our present strength to our ancestry, and still more to the great Father of us all. Especially is this true of the lives which are peculiarly rich and helpful. These are the elect lives for whose efficiency the generations have been preparing under the guidance of God.

With many of the best men of our times Professor CRITTENDEN could trace his lineage through a sober, hard-working, and devout ancestry. He came from a rural community where the life of the people, during the early part of this century, was well fitted to develop the best traits of character. There was no excess of wealth and very little severe poverty. Toil was known to be a divine ordination. The Word of God was an open volume in every home, and the family altar witnessed the morning and evening sacrifices. The sanctuary and the school-house stood side by side. Attention to education was an evidence of a determination to excel. The opportunities of life were prized by those who meant to use them. From scenes such as these our friend went forth to consecrate himself to the grandest of all vocations, even that which secured the activity of the Son of God during the three years of His incarnate ministry. In a Christian spirit he entered upon and conducted his work. With clear perception he grasped the fact, so often in debate, that Christianity means the best culture of spirit, soul, and body; that the thought of Christ marches ahead of the centuries; and that no true science no pure art, can be antagonistic to the religion of the cross. He was a Christian educator. This is his rare distinction. For more than half a century he maintained a position—and one of which he had a right to be proud—in the front rank of his associates. From the institutions under his charge hundreds of noble women have gone forth to adorn homes, to reproduce his work in other schools, and to evangelize the world. Upon multitudes of graduates he has conferred the degrees of honor which this illustrious foundation grants: and now he has received his degree from our Lord, whom he has served so well.

> "I hear again the Master's simple words,
> So low, so sweet, conferring Thy degree:
> 'Of such My kingdom is; let none forbid
> His coming unto me.'"

Thus the grain ripened and its maturity was reached. The fruitage was freely given year by year. An abundant usefulness was realized. Then the reaper came, and the harvest of a new planting was gathered in by God. With well-rounded character, with a rich Christian consciousness, the scholar, teacher, friend, and father was transported to the "sweet fields beyond the swelling flood," where strength and beauty appear forever in perpetual bloom. There is no autumn there, and no decay; no chill of winter, and no storms.

Therefore we are here not with the sorrow of despair, but with the chastened sorrow of a grief which laments the absence of one beloved and honored, which rejoices that a life has been grandly lived on earth, which believes that heaven is now the sphere of activity of a spirit prepared for its purity and joy.

He has "come to his grave as a shock of corn cometh
in in his season."

> " Do you mourn when another star
>   Shines out from the glorious sky ?
> Do you weep when the sound of war
>   And the rush of conflict die ?
> Why then should your tears flow down,
>   And your hearts seem sorely riven,
> For another gem in the Saviour's crown,
>   And another soul in heaven ?"

DR. STORRS'S ADDRESS,

as reported by the Brooklyn *Eagle*, was substantially as follows:

I met him [Dr. CRITTENDEN] first in the building which preceded the present structure, nearly thirty-eight years ago, before I had come to Brooklyn to reside. He seemed then in delicate health rather than robust, and as if any shock of disease might strike him fatally. At different times since he has been feeble, though always cheerful and never complaining. Still at different times one meeting him in the street in cold or stormy weather might easily feel that he could hardly bear such common exposure; and yet he had passed the usual limit of life, had even passed the fourscore years, and, as was said recently by President Hill of President Hopkins, " he had borrowed twelve years of eternity." A long life is not necessarily a blessed life, but his has been, as has been said, a peculiarly happy one; yet my own pastoral relation to him has covered the years in which repeated and sore sorrows have fallen upon him: in the long illness and final death of his accomplished and beloved daughter; in the protracted illness, followed also by death, of his cherished and honored wife, in whom always his heart rejoiced and rested; and only a few weeks since in the sudden illness and death of a beloved grandchild. He has been under these shadows in these recent years, and yet his life has been a happy one in the midst of it all—partly by reason of his freshness and vivacity of force which continued with him to the last, and of his genial and kindly cheerfulness and warm affection which never failed. He was always happy, too, in his own work. Many men perform the duties entrusted to them feeling them a burden. He was always enthusiastic as a teacher, never leaving the school until the last day of the term had arrived, returning to it promptly and gladly on the first day of the new year. His enthusiasm in his work never abated and never ceased. He was especially happy in his home, full of tenderness and full of gladness in the society of those who made it beautiful and precious. He was happy beyond most in the kindly relations which connected him with many of the living here and afar, and in the recollections of many of the dead with whom he had had cordial and affectionate relations, whom he delighted to recall, and of whom he was never weary of speaking. Above all he was happy in his firm and unwavering Christian faith which he had received in childhood, and which he maintained unfalteringly to the end; never staggered before any mystery, and never yielding before any assault, but always maintaining the robust and energetic convictions of the truth which had been his from early life. The Gospel to him brought life and immortality to light. It showed the God of creation as the God of redemption. It showed the power of the regenerating spirit and the clear, lofty promise of the life eternal. In it he had gladness and assurance always; from it he drew his comfort in the darkest hour of grief. The shadow of death which was in his household was again and again illumined by the light of the promised immortality. It has been said that the promise of the Old Testament is worldly welfare; that the promise of the New Testament is tribulation. Both were fulfilled to him, but he felt that the tribulation came from the same loving divine kindness which had sent all the other blessings of his life. And even in sorrow he was strong and at rest in the confidence of God's love. His life was eminently a useful life, far wider in reach of influence than would have seemed probable when he first came to the city. The city itself had then but sixty thousand inhabitants. It was secluded more than now from the general life of the country. The Academy to which he came, as matched against this noble Institution, was comparatively small. It might be anticipated that his work would reach usefully many of the misses and young ladies of the town itself, but hardly that it should reach to all parts of the land and be a presence and a power in multitudes of homes throughout the country. Yet this he has accomplished. As a teacher he has been stimulating and suggestive, stirring the minds of pupils with many eager questions, as well as imparting knowledge. As Principal of the Institute he has administered its affairs with rare faithfulness and discretion, so that among all the teachers who at different times have been associated with him here there has been, so far as I am aware, no serious jar or break of harmony. He has given moral impulse and guidance as well as intellectual instruction. His heart was more in the religious services of this chapel than in any other specific department of instruction in the class-room, and many have received from him impulses to goodness and the beauty and faith of consecration. Around his coffin as a centre are

gathered to-day the remembrances and the honoring
regard of the older and the younger alike. Those who
are now themselves in advanced life received from
him instruction in their youth, while those who are
still children here have been equally conscious of his
power to bless. He has built his own spirit into the
Institute itself. His portrait may hang upon the can-
vas in the library, but the real image of his mind and
character will be found hereafter in the institution
which for almost forty years he has so efficiently
guided and controlled.

Of a life so rounded, so prolonged and finished in
happiness and usefulness we can have no words of regret to speak. It seems, as one looks back upon it
from the end, like a long day of summer, clouded at
intervals, yet for the most part bright, and closing in
the beauties and peace of sunset. His way of life did
not lead into the sear and yellow leaf, yet he had all
which should accompany old age, as honor, love,
obedience, and troops of friends. We are here only
to learn such lessons of his life as he would teach, if
his dumb tongue again could speak. Certainly he
would tell us that the source of happiness in him, of
culture both of mind and heart, of power over others
for their blessing, had been in the Gospel of the Son
of God; that by its truths his mind had received its
highest illumination; that by its promises his spirit
had been cheered and lifed from the earth; that in its
hopes his joy had been, and in their fulfilment was
now his eternal happiness and rest. He would tell
us that the loving-kindness of the Heavenly Father,
which had been with him all his life and with him at
its end, was now more manifest than ever amid the
wonders of immortality.

Quoting some of the Scripture passages which Dr. CRITTENDEN had delighted most to dwell upon, the speaker concluded by saying:

At the very end of life, when he had scarcely strength to speak, he wished to be lifted and supported that he might say one word more to those around him, and the word which came feebly to his dying lips was that word " Love,"—the word which is the secret of all the Bible, which was the motive of Christ's mission and the power of His life; which is the element of holiness, and which is the source of victory in death—which is the life of life eternal. It cannot but be that a spirit so genial and active, so affectionate and reverent, shall find immortality a sphere for culture and for work continuing and unlimited.

It is the privilege of age that more of those associations with our life are gathered within the veil than tarry here. When the little child dies we sometimes feel or fear that the realms into which it enters may be strange, that it will meet few there whom it has known on earth. The Saviour assures us of such that "their angels do always behold the face of My Father in heaven." And human friends who have not known them on earth, we fondly trust, will know and cherish them for our sake. But when one passes, like our friend, into that other sphere, how many shall there be to welcome him as he comes ! Those whose faces had ceased to shine upon him on the earth now radiant in celestial light ; those whose voices had been silenced in this world, now ringing

with the heavenly music, shall meet and greet him
with the fulness of heavenly love.

.   .   .   .

We look upon this life as not closed but con-
summated.

DR. TALMAGE'S ADDRESS.

On the Friday following the funeral Rev. Dr. T. DeWitt Talmage, at his weekly prayer-meeting, gave the following beautiful tribute to the late Principal of the Packer Collegiate Institute:

The city of Brooklyn and many people all over the land sighed heavily when they heard this week that Professor CRITTENDEN of the Packer Institute was dead. We never had a kinder heart or nobler nature in this city of Brooklyn. His life-work was to make the people wise, happy, and good. Forming his acquaintance at my coming here, I began by thinking well of him at the start, and I have thought better and better of him all the way. I am so sad that he is gone. How we shall miss him from our social circles and our churches! What an educator of the young, himself the grandest lesson of what industry and kindliness and the religion of the Lord Jesus Christ may achieve! What an impression on the daughters of America—thousands of them passing under his benediction! When will the life of the good man cease? Not while the world stands; for who shall estimate the widening influence, from generation to generation, and from age to age, in all parts of the land? I find the matrons, some of them already silver-haired, telling of what he did to give them nobler views of life and fit them for the spheres they now occupy.

I never thought him old, he was so young in all his sympathies, so buoyant in his spirits, so anticipative of good yet to be accomplished; but bereavement and watching with the sick, and many years of absorbing application to hard work, will tell at last, and these Friday-evening shadows lie on Professor CRITTEN-DEN's grave. The whole city rises up to do him honor. All who speak of him find their words melting into tears. No one asks whether he was ready. Such a question would have been an absurdity. You might as well ask a soldier at the close of an exhaustive war if he would like to go to his family at the homestead; you might as well ask a sea-captain, after being tossed on a long voyage, if he would like to see Barnegat lighthouse. A useful life well closed and multitudes pronouncing his eulogium. Call them professors or school-teachers or educators, as you may, what a mission for all those who direct the rising generation on the high paths of integrity and honor! Many of these instructors on incompetent salaries and in poorly ventilated apartments, ofttimes disheartened with the refractory dispositions under their charge, and toiling with little recognition on the part of a sometimes critical public, may now learn that rest comes at last; all anxieties hushed forever. "Blessed are the dead who die in the Lord; they rest from their labors, and their works do follow them."

ALONZO CRITTENDEN—may his name be held in everlasting remembrance!

III.

Extracts from Letters of Condolence written to
Mr. Edward Crittenden and Family after
the Death of Dr. Crittenden.

When the telegram reached Asheville announcing the passing away of the elder of the two old friends, the younger gathered up his failing energies and dictated to his wife the following letter of sympathy and condolence:

ASHEVILLE, N. C., January 26, 1883.

My DEAR FRIENDS:

The news of your dear father's death did not reach me until this morning. Notwithstanding the days of anxious suspense and your kind letters warning us of the approaching end, it seemed sudden and startling, as such news always does.

Can it be that he is really gone?

From my sick-bed I look through the open window and can see the lovely landscape, with its mountain, valley, and river bathed in the glorious light of this southern sun. The whole heavens are overspread with the purest light, and through its deep sapphire I can almost see the crystal pavement where the redeemed walk. And *he* is among the shining throng that crowd those golden streets! We would not bring him back.

.   .   .   .

I *was* near him in spirit during all those days of sinking. . . . You know how I loved him. It is seldom that two lives have been so intimately knit together as ours. For more than thirty years we have known and loved each other. It is hard to part, and the gloom that settles on my own spirit assures me that life can never again be to me quite what it was.

But why should I dwell on my own sorrow in the presence of your overshadowing grief? I have lost a friend, you a father! How my heart has gone out to you during the swift and terrible events of this strange winter! But, my dear friends, we are in God's hands, and He is too wise to err. Let us trust him for His grace and follow where He leads. He will surely bring us into the light.

Affectionately and sincerely yours,

D. G. EATON.

January 27, 1883.

We are all greatly pained to learn of the death of your honored and beloved father. A few days ago I heard of his sickness, and I was hoping to find time to go over to Brooklyn and call upon him. But I have been so closely occupied that I have not been free to go as I desired. I may not see him again until we meet among the saints in heaven.

Dear old man! His life here was a benediction. He came to us with a smile and a word of cheer, and he left us in the same way. Few reach his years and retain his activity. His conversation was as fresh as that of a man of forty, and so was his sympathy. He numbered the years until he had counted more than fourscore, and yet his heart was the heart of a child. To me he will always be a pleasant memory. I am grateful that I have had even a little of the friendship of so great and good a man.

He waited, lonesome and sad after God called your mother. He knew that the time of his own departure could not be far distant. His lamp was trimmed and burning; when his summons came, he went home with great joy.

HENRY M. BOOTH.

I was greatly pained to read this morning the announcement of your father's death. He is mourned by friends who had known him longer than I; but no one can have known him more agreeably. The world seems poorer by his going out of it.

I find it to be impossible to attend the funeral. So you will please excuse me where I find it so difficult to excuse myself, and accept the assurance of my sincerest sympathy.

Yours very truly,

ROSWELL D. HITCHCOCK.

WASHINGTON, D.C., January 24.

Your telegram has been forwarded from Cambridge. At length my dear life-long friend has gone to join your dear mother. . .

How full of years and of never-ceasing good deeds, blessing all with whom he came in contact, your father's life has been! He has had a most lasting influence on my whole life. It could scarcely have been more penetrating if I had been your brother. E. N. HORSFORD.

MONTREAL, March 11.

I feel most grateful to you for so promptly writing. The death to us has been terribly sudden, not having heard of your father being otherwise than in usual health. I had a most kind letter dated November 9th, written, as he said, by a borrowed hand, referring me to John, 1st chapter, 13th and 14th verses, and cordially urging us to trust the Lord. . . I shall never cease to regret that my children could not have known personally one so tenderly and pleasantly associated with my early life, and one to whom I feel I owe so much. Very many thanks for the photograph, which I think very good of the dear face which will never be effaced from my memory.

H. I. W.

50 FIRST PLACE, January 24.

The gap which the death of your honored father has made calls forth my deepest sympathy for yourself and your dear family. When through long years I look back to the just path which he took for his pilgrimage, and remember with what earnestness he filled that path with good deeds, and how the very beauty of his character caused others to love wisdom, I feel thankful that such a man has lived; and am sure that though he is now with the blessed ones in glory, and away from us, yet his influence will be long felt by many thankful hearts. K. D.

ROME, February 24.

You and your family have our very sincere sympathies in the death of your father, the news of which reached us last week. Your father is associated with my earliest remembrances, and for forty years my associations with him and your mother have been to me sources of the greatest interest and pleasure. Your mother was a noble woman, towering above other women; kindly, affectionate, and true. A. M. O.

January 23, 1883.

The many years we have been associated with your dear father makes us feel we have lost a personal friend and must mingle our tears with yours on this sad occasion.

Not sad to him, for to go into the presence of the dear Saviour whom he loved and so faithfully served, and to join the loved ones gone before, is not sad, with him "instant death was instant glory." No more weariness, no more suffering, no more pain, but everlasting rest and joy.

Yours in deep sympathy,

H. J. and E. G.

Our thoughts and sympathies have been with you all very much these past days. So much has gone from my life in the loss of one of my best and kindest of friends that it seems very lonely even for me, for Mr. CRITTENDEN has done more in moulding me for my life-work, and in helpful encouragement in it, than any one else. The memory of his love and kindness will always be very precious. I. P. W.

My best friend was your father; and when I heard of his sickness, I was in hopes that he would be spared, and at some future day I might make him feel proud of his ward.

A. J. FOX.

IV.

Resolutions of Sympathy.

MINUTES AND RESOLUTIONS ADOPTED BY

THE PRESIDENT AND BOARD OF TRUSTEES

THE EVENING AFTER DR. CRITTENDEN'S DEATH.

The announcement of the death this morning of ALONZO CRIT-
·TENDEN, the venerable and long honored Principal of the Packer
Collegiate Institute, is received by the Board of Trustees with
profound sensibility. The successful head of great schools for
higher female education for more than half a century, and of our
Brooklyn Female Academy, and its corporate successor, the
Packer Collegiate Institute, for nearly two score of years, he had
attained the highest rank and distinction as an upright and skilful
educator and administrator. Although he had passed his fourscore years before his late illness just terminated by his lamented
death, his eye had not become dim nor his natural force abated.
Under his wise, vigilant, and efficient administration, the Albany
Female Academy, the Brooklyn Female Academy, and the Packer
Collegiate Institute successively prospered and attained a foremost place among the academic institutions of the country. Alert,
punctual, judicious and firm in his headship, he formed, developed, and directed numerous accomplished teachers, and kindled
the studious zeal while he won the affectionate confidence and regard of the thousands of scholars he had helped to train for
elevated and useful lives. The members of this Board, responsi-
bly and intimately associated with him for so many years in the care
and direction of this Institute, bear emphatic testimony to the integrity of his character, the blameless purity of his life, the un-
sparing zeal with which he devoted himself to his duties as principal, and the rare tact, judgment, and temper with which he fulfilled the often difficult and always laborious trusts committed to
him. Teachers and scholars now in this Institution have heard,
and thousands of both who have been taught or trained in it, and
are now ministering to the peace and joy of many homes in this
and other cities and States, will hear of his death with tears and
tender regrets. With a profound conviction of his rare worth
and of our great loss, we unite in the acclaim, "Well done, good
and faithful servant!"

The Board directs this minute to be entered upon its permanent records, and that a copy of it, with an expression of our
warmest sympathy, be sent to the bereaved family of our late
honored and regretted associate and friend.

Resolved, That this Board will attend the funeral of Mr. CRIT-
TENDEN, and that it is the desire of the Board that the funeral services be solemnized in our chapel.

FACULTY OF THE PACKER COLLEGIATE INSTITUTE
ADOPTED THE DAY OF DR. CRITTENDEN'S DEATH.

Only death teaches us to know the full measure of the life it closes. It is a grand thing to outlast the fourscore years assigned as the earthly limit of human existence, to look with undimmed eye and unclouded intellect from the mountain-top of old age, back upon the ascending path of an honorable and well-spent life, then forward and upward, with confidence and faith to another and higher life for which the gathering years have been passed in preparation.

Our beloved President, Dr. ALONZO CRITTENDEN, has been taken from us in the full ripeness of a well-rounded life. His was a life devoted to the cause of education, and of which the Packer Collegiate Institute is the living monument. As an educator, he sought ever to develop not intellect alone, but character. He operated not merely through the medium of instruction, but yet more through that of exquisite tact, ready sympathy, kindly geniality, moral force, and quick personal magnetism. None, whether teachers or pupils, could come within the sound of his voice without feeling the prompt influence of his personality. Clear in his ideas, ready and reliable in judgment, always kind and considerate, whether in giving advice or conveying reproof, his power as a guide made his administration one that was marked by cheerful and positive accordance in aim among those over whom he was placed as president, and singular freedom from friction in the management of details. He has impressed his individuality upon hundreds of teachers and thousands of students throughout the existence of this institution, with which he has been identified from its first organization. To each of us he was a personal friend in whom there was no guile, on whose sincerity perfect reliance could be placed, and whose rich experience and ready adaptability made his advice ever worthy of confidence. We mourn him as our President, but equally do we mourn him as our friend.

Since it has pleased the Giver of all life to take back that which is His own, be it resolved, by the teachers of the Packer Collegiate Institute,

That the death of our loved and honored President, Dr. ALONZO CRITTENDEN, is a calamity which fills us with deepest grief, and before which we bow with humility, realizing the loss as one which cannot be filled, but recognizing the Power that has limited the years of man, even when these are wholly spent in bestowing happiness and blessing upon all.

That our warmest sympathy is offered to the bereaved family, whose loss is our loss and whose sore affliction we share in bitter sorrow.

That this preamble and these resolutions be entered upon the record of the Packer Collegiate Institute, that a copy be sent to the family of him whose death we mourn, and that a copy be furnished for publication in the columns of the Brooklyn *Daily Eagle.*

> W. Le C. Stevens,
> S. K. Cook,
> M. E. Thalheimer,
> Charlotte Titcomb,
> *Committee.*

RESOLUTIONS UNANIMOUSLY ADOPTED BY THE

ASSOCIATE ALUMNÆ OF THE PACKER COLLEGIATE INSTITUTE,

JANUARY 25, 1883.

Whereas, It has pleased Almighty God to take from us by death the honored President of our Alma Mater, identified with its interests from its organization and endeared to all of its graduates by so many ties of affection and respect ;

Resolved, That in the death of ALONZO CRITTENDEN the Packer Collegiate Institute has lost not only one of its firmest friends, but one who, by his high character, purity of life, earnestness and persistency of purpose, and marked ability as an educator, has raised the Institute to rank among the foremost of those devoted to the education of women.

Resolved, That in view of the fact that he earnestly and intelligently advocated the cause of the higher education of women at a time when it had few advocates, and devoted a long and honored life to its practical attainment, he is worthy of the respect and grateful remembrance of all true women.

Resolved, That we, the graduates of the Packer Collegiate Institute, recognizing the influence of his high personal character and love of letters, and his earnest and untiring efforts for the advancement of those under his charge, as well as his kindly sympathy and his interest in our success, feel that in his death we have lost a personal friend.

Resolved, That as a mark of respect for his memory, the Alumnæ attend his funeral in a body.

Resolved, That we deeply sympathize with his family in their bereavement.

Resolved, That a copy of these resolutions be sent to the family, and that they be published in the daily papers.

> M. A. S. KITCHELL, *President Assoc. Alumnæ.*
> ADELINA BIERCK, *Secretary.*

BROOKLYN COLLEGIATE AND POLYTECHNIC IN-STITUTE,

JANUARY 27, 1883.   •

The Trustees of the Brooklyn Collegiate and Polytechnic Insti-tute, recalling with gratitude its early history and the intimate relations which have always existed between this Institution and the Packer Collegiate Institute, have learned with deep sorrow of the death, on Monday the 22d inst, of Professor ALONZO CRITTEN-DEN, President of its Faculty.

Called nearly a third of a century ago to the supervision of the Brooklyn Female Academy, and later to that of its successor the Packer Collegiate Institute, Professor CRITTENDEN gave the ripest years of his manhood and all the treasures of a liberal and refined scholarship to the building up of these Institutions, and by his unremitting zeal and unstinted services secured for each a standing among our citizens that has reflected honor upon himself not only, but upon our city and State as well.

After a prolonged life devoted to the higher education of the young women of our city, and of those drawn hither by the repu-tation he secured for the Institute, he has passed away from our companionship, leaving behind him the fragrant memory of an earnest life successfully spent in the highest culture of the intel-lects and hearts of those who have been placed under his care, who will gratefully cherish the remembrance of his deep interest in them and encouragement of them in their individual efforts and attainments.

In grateful appreciation of the purity of his life, of the integrity of his character, of his earnest devotion to the higher training of those who in ever-increasing numbers have been confided to his teaching, of his genial companionship, and of his healthfulness in every educational and elevating instrumentality, the Trustees and Faculty of this Institute desire to place upon its permanent records their expression of their respect and esteem, and of their pro-found sympathy with the family and friends of our respected co-laborer in the cause of education, and with the Trustees and officers of the Institute over which so long and so efficiently he has pre-sided.

In thus uniting with the whole community in our tribute of re-spect for a departed townsman, our sympathies are most tenderly invoked in behalf of his intimate and cherished friend and assist-ant for the entire term of his presidency, Professor Darwin G. Eaton, who is now absent from his professorship, seeking under medical advisement and in a less rigorous climate the restoration of his health.

Universally respected and beloved for his scientific and literary attainments, and for the beauty of his life and character, we extend to him the assurances of our sincere regard and sympathy and our warmest wishes for his speedy recovery, and for his early return to the sphere of his prolonged and appreciated labors.

The President and Treasurer of the Board are requested to have this memorial engrossed upon its records, and copies thereof transmitted to the family of the late President CRITTENDEN, to Professor Darwin G. Eaton at Asheville, N. C., and to the Board of Trustees of the Packer Collegiate Institute.

I. H. FROTHINGHAM, *President.*
TASKER H. MARVIN, *Treasurer.*

RESOLUTIONS ADOPTED BY THE

ADELPHI ACADEMY.

At a special meeting of the Faculty of the Adelphi Academy held this 24th day of January, 1883, the following resolutions were adopted :

Whereas, Our Heavenly Father in His infinite wisdom and love has called from his earthly home Dr. ALONZO CRITTENDEN, President of the Packer Collegiate Institute ;

Resolved, That we tender our common and deep sympathy to the family of the deceased, and to the officers and teachers of the Institute which his spirit has guided for so many years.

Resolved, That in his patient and warm friendship, in his faithfulness and earnestness as a teacher, in his untiring and courageous efforts as an educator, and in his conserving and guiding genius as the presiding officer of large institutions of learning, we find consolation for all the changes which are common to this life.

Resolved, That while we recognize in our late co laborer a pioneer in the cause of higher education for women, an able exponent and defender of higher education in general, and an illustrious example for all teachers ; we are rendered most deeply grateful for that simple manhood, that pure and sturdy character, that Christian love and charity which silently but effectively moulded the lives of all his pupils and made him in reality a ruler among mankind, and a source of light and hope to all.

S. G. TAYLOR, *President of Faculty.*
W. C. PECKHAM, *Secretary.*